A paperback original

NOW YOU SEE ME...

Praise for Emma Beal
NOW YOU SEE ME...

Would highly recommend this book it's a brilliant read, could not put it down!

This book sends shivers down your spine! It's fast-paced, full of ups and downs, twists and turns. You find yourself praying that Jade will be free, that she doesn't suffer anymore, and just when you think she has, it starts all over again! You almost don't want to turn the page because you fear for her on every level.

This book is so well written and makes a gripping read. You just want the best for Jade and for her to escape and turn her life around and be free.

Absolutely fabulous read, binge-read it Sunday morning. Couldn't put it down (to the point where I burned my breakfast) This author can write!!

Loved this book from start to finish but definitely didn't expect the ending (well done jade lol) I was hoping for that kind of result all the way through. I liked the fact that it was set in places I am very familiar with, it felt like I was watching it rather than reading it. Emma Beal's books are worth reading , try them!

I have read all of Emma's books and this is bar far the best. I was totally gripped from page 1 and it didn't disappoint. What an excellent read. If you haven't read a book by Emma then you are truly missing out.

BY EMMA L BEAL

(1) NOW YOU SEE ME...

WWW.EMMALBEALAUTHOR.COM

www.emmalbealauthor.com

A Paperback Original 2022

First published in Great Britain by Emma L Beal 2022

Copyright © EmmaLBeal2022

Hope is the thing with feathers

"Hope" is the thing with feathers -
That perches in the soul -
And sings the tune without the words -
And never stops - at all -

And sweetest - in the Gale - is heard -
And sore must be the storm -
That could abash the little Bird
That kept so many warm -

I've heard it in the chillest land -
And on the strangest Sea -
Yet - never - in Extremity,
It asked a crumb - of me.

By Emily Dickinson

REAL STRENGTH IS FOUND BEHIND CLOSED DOORS.

NOW YOU SEE ME...

Emma L Beal

CONTENTS

PART ONE
WHERE IT ALL BEGAN

PART TWO
MY PRESENT, MY FUTURE

PART THREE
NEW BEGINNINGS

PART FOUR
THE PAST RETURNS...

PART ONE

WHERE IT ALL BEGAN...

*'**C**'mon Jade, it's only a few drinks, and you never know, you might finally meet a handsome stranger that will change your life forever.'*

Those words were spoken to me three years ago, with a theatrical wink and a cheeky smile, as my best friend Heidi had thrown clothes haphazardly from my wardrobe in a desperate bid to find me the perfect *catch-a-fella* outfit, and as I had groaned loudly at the injustice of not being permitted to stay happily single.

Heidi, my best friend since primary school knew me better than anyone. We looked completely different, me a short brunette, her a leggy blonde – yet we were always asked if we were sisters – so alike were we in many ways. So, I knew that she understood why I didn't want to go out, why I wasn't interested in meeting anybody new – after all, she was the one who picked up the pieces after what Damon had done to me – but I also knew that this was her way of helping me break the gloom that I had fallen into regarding men. It didn't mean that I had to be happy about it though. My last relationship hadn't ended so well, and I can admit, somewhat ashamedly that I did not handle things in a particularly calm and collected manner.

11

But you see, Damon, he didn't exactly leave me in a position that screamed tranquillity, a mutual decision, a truce.

No.

Damon lied and schemed and plotted behind my back, he had so many other women stored in his mobile phone that I'm surprised he didn't get himself confused, but liars don't do they?

Their craft is so fine-tuned that the lies aren't even lies anymore, they are just blank spaces, empty words, something to be brushed aside, non-consequential, a joke!

I had found Damon in *our* home, in *our* bed (*yes, we were that serious*) with a woman that I had never seen before, and I had reacted badly.

The anger that had burst from me had been immense, and I had frightened myself a little.

I had thrown things; I had screamed, and I had rather stupidly threatened to kill them both. It hadn't been my finest hour.

The woman hiding in our bathroom did at least have the decency to look apologetic, but we all knew that that was only because they had been caught, and her screaming and blubbering that she was calling the police had done nothing to calm me down. Damon had begged for forgiveness, all but forgetting about his little piece on the side who was still cowering, naked in our ensuite bathroom, but I couldn't forgive him.

How could he expect me to?

He had moved out that night.

It was only after he had left and all trace of him was removed from my sight that I had broken down. I had cried so hard that my chest hurt, and I had screamed so loudly that I was sure the police would arrive, certain that there was a murder underway. But they had not arrived – and so I remained alone in my despair.

I started shaking then. Shaking so violently that I could not breathe. I was broken.

It took me a long time to get over what Damon did, I was emotionally invested in him, I was emotionally invested in us, but he had destroyed it all, he had destroyed our future - and so now you see why being single worked just fine for me.

Single people do not get cheated on.

Single people do not have to worry about opening their bedroom doors.

Single people are free of heartache.

I wish that I had stayed single because I was happy.

I was free!

Had I known back then just what those words would lead to, I would have shoved those wretched clothes back into the wardrobe and refused to leave the house – but hindsight is a wonderful thing isn't it – because I had no idea what was heading my way.

No idea at all.

The Dirty Rabbit bar had been heaving as Heidi, Nicky, Jessica, Gordon *(Heidi's older brother)* and I had pushed our way through the large red double doors, looking eagerly for a place to sit and take the weight off of our painfully high heeled feet.

Nicky looked sensational as always in her cut-off denim shorts, pink vest top and cowboy boots, her brown hair brushed until it gleamed – whereas Jessica, the more fashionably adventurous of us all was rocking purple tights, a bright pink dress and *Irregular Choice* shoes, alongside her recently dyed blue hair – we didn't know why it worked, but on Jessica it just did!

Heidi was classy as always in her simple black dress and silver sandals, and I was wearing blue jeans and a gold sparkly top with gold high-heeled sandals - and I was extremely thankful for Heidi's simple yet cute choice.

14

I'll admit that as soon as I had seen the queue at the bar and the lack of seating available, I had been mentally preparing my excuses to leave, but Nicky, flirtatious and unreserved as always, had, with a wink and a smile, managed to squeeze us onto a table full of *suits*, it was then that I had known that the night could not possibly be redeemed.

What could any of us possibly have in common with city men? We all worked in retail for crying out loud, and Whitby, North Yorkshire, wasn't exactly a bustling metropolis, it was in fact a world away from spreadsheets, mergers and acquisitions!

They no doubt got off on big sales and commissions, whereas we counted ourselves blessed if we managed to stack the baked beans and quirky tourist souvenirs quickly enough to get us an early finish.

Smiling awkwardly, I squeezed my way past three incredibly well-groomed men, who were equally as incredibly drunk, avoiding eye contact as much as I could. Striking up a conversation had certainly not been on my agenda that evening.

I had already decided that I would stay for a few drinks and then excuse myself. I had known that Heidi would be disappointed, so eager had she been to see me set up romantically, but I had been happy being single and could not understand why that needed to change. I enjoyed my own space, my own rules, my freedom, and had seen no solid reason why letting a man into my life to change that would have been beneficial to me, but Heidi had been determined, and I had learnt quickly that sometimes it was just easier to appease her appetite for romance, even if it went against everything that I wanted for myself.

Jessica and Nicky had already taken over a small patch of space and turned it into a makeshift dancefloor and had been having a whale of a time, while Gordon, all six foot two of him had been busy keeping a watchful eye on his younger sister Heidi, ensuring that the *suit* she was busy chatting away to didn't step over any of the boundaries that he had mentally set for her.

Gordon, just to set the record straight wasn't a party pooper, and his protectiveness in no way stopped him from having a good time, but Heidi had fallen foul of a domineering bully of a man not so long ago, and Gordon had promised that he would never again let another man lay hands upon his little sister.

Gordon doesn't actually live in Whitby, but he visits regularly. His home is in Leeds, which he says is the perfect place to run his rather large property empire from.

I don't know much about the buying and selling of homes, but Gordon does, and that's why he is incredibly successful and incredibly well-off. You wouldn't know it though; he isn't pompous or snobbish in any way at all. He's one of us. Looking around I had become suddenly aware of the reason that the place was so busy, it was because there was a hen party, and the bride-to-be was having a whale of a time crooning to *By the light of the silvery moon*, that one of her fellow hens had brought up on her mobile phone, much to the distaste of the regular punters.

Resplendent in her plastic tiara and pink sash, the bride was clearly three sheets to the wind, as she danced merrily around, letting everybody know *(who didn't already)* that she – Freya Merriweather, was to be married in three days, and that her husband to be was *just so perfect!*

I had to wonder, as I watched her, so happy, so infatuated – would I ever feel that way again?

Would I ever feel such burning passion for a person that I would want to shout it out to everyone that would listen – and those, of course, that wouldn't?

Downing my drink, I had laughed quietly to myself – who needed love anyway?

Somehow two hours had passed, and I couldn't quite

recall how – I wasn't having a good time, I had been busy people-watching since I arrived – had anybody even noticed that I wasn't *quite in the room*?

'Get you another?' a deep, smooth voice had asked, 'white wine, isn't it?'

'No, thank you.' I smiled, taking in the man before me. He was good-looking, extremely well-built, and extremely tall.

With his dazzling smile, dark hair and *Hugo Boss* aftershave – he was a million miles away from my type of man. At only five foot two myself, I tended to steer away from men that I had to physically look up to. 'I'm heading home soon, so…'

'So soon?' he had chuckled, as he took a seat next to me, 'not a proper party animal then, like your mates?' he questioned while nodding over at Jessica and Nicky, who were a lot less sober than when we had first arrived, and who were proving to be a big hit not only with two local men but also their rather interesting rendition of *Come on Eileen*. 'Are they always like *that*?'

'Always like what? They're just having fun.'

'I'm sure they are.' He had laughed, 'But will it just be fun later when those fellas want a little more than flirting?'

Stunned I turned to face him, 'Are you saying that women

can't flirt without it leading to sex?'

'Well, they are really going for it over there. Any hotblooded male would naturally assume…'

'Naturally assume what? That because a woman is having a good time it must mean she's easy?'

'I didn't mean to offend you.' He sighed, downing his beer and reaching for the next one that he had lined up on the table.

'I'm sure you didn't.' I had scowled, staring over at Gordon to come and save me.

Judgemental men I most certainly did not need. We had all learnt a hard lesson via Heidi, and none of us was open to that kind of car wreck in our life.

'Everything okay over here?' Gordon had asked, towering over the city boy.

Gordon himself was a large man, and most people tended to assume that his height and his bulk meant that he was either always up for a fight, or someone to be avoided. He was neither of course, not that he ever let anyone outside of our social circle know that.

'Ah c'mon, I didn't mean anything by it, can't I just buy you a drink and start over?'

'No, really, I'm fine.' I had muttered, eager to get away. 'You have a *fun* evening though.'

19

'I'll walk you home.' Gordon had smiled at me, understanding my need to be away.

'Oh, you don't have to do that.' I had responded flippantly, 'I'll be fine, honestly.'

Still eyeballing the man, Gordon had shaken his head, 'I'm walking you home, you don't know what weirdos are out there.'

Grabbing my handbag, I had managed to squeeze myself past the rest of the people at the table, relieved to finally be out of the corner, when I swear, I had heard him mutter '*Bitch*' under his breath.

Turning to face him, I asked what he had just said, but he shrugged and smiled innocently at me, denying that he had even uttered a word.

But I swear even to this day that he called me a bitch – somehow though, in the many months that were to follow, I convinced myself that I had misheard, that he didn't in fact say a word - but now?

Now I know that he did, and I wish that I had listened to my head and not been overruled by my stupid heart, because my head would not have led me straight into the arms of the devil.

The first text message arrived two months after our initial

doomed forever meeting, whereby I discovered that Jessica, drunk and eager to please had handed out my mobile phone number to the most ignorant man in the bar, *Eric Sawyer*, who was desperate to apologise for his outlandish behaviour.

I had ignored it.

As I had ignored the seven that followed.

Now I cannot explain why I eventually relented and responded to Eric, but I did, and it was the start of what I believed at the time to be something wonderful.

Sober Eric was nothing like the piggish neanderthal that I had encountered at *The Dirty Rabbit* many months ago, he was, in fact, sweet, caring and a total gentleman. So, spurred on by Heidi and her ridiculous notions of romance I decided to bite the bullet and meet with him once more.

Eric didn't live in Whitby, he was as I had already worked out in the bar, a city boy through and through. Originally from Hornsea, he had moved to Leeds to pursue his career in accountancy, and his hard work must have paid off, as by the time we met he was the very proud owner of his own business, *Sawyer Inc.*

His city centre apartment was chic, minimalistic, cool and sophisticated and also overlooked the River Aire, which had looked rather charming in the photographs that he had sent me, but secretly I knew that I would never swap my well lived in, cosy home, or view of the fishing harbour and North Sea for anything.

Whitby was in my mind the perfect place to live in the whole world. With its one hundred and ninety-nine steps leading up to *St Mary's Church* and the *Abbey*, which were used back in the day for funerals – no mean feat I'm sure for the pall bearers, however, there are regular stopping points along the way in the form of wooden benches.

It is also said that the one hundred and ninety-nine steps were used as a test of faith for those who wanted to worship at St Mary's Church – by climbing them you were proving that you were faithful.

The Abbey itself, used in Bram Stoker's *Dracula* novel, was destroyed during a Viking invasion around 870 A.D but was eventually refounded as a Benedictine priory in 1077, amongst others during the years that followed. The Abbey was complete as late as 1711, but now only the ruins remain – it is however still one of the main attractions in Whitby, and despite it no longer standing complete and in its full glory, it is still a stunning sight to behold.

There was also a woman that many locals believed to be a witch, and she went by the name of *Mad Maggie*.

22

Maggie, it would seem had the ability to predict deaths, and instilled so much fear into the locals, that selling her lucky charms and talismans made her quite a profitable living.

Maggie also predicted her own death and foretold that a fierce storm would wreak havoc upon Whitby on the day of her death – it did – so maybe Maggie really was a witch after all.

There is also *Captain Cook*, *Whitby Goth Weekend*, *Whitby Jet*, the *Whale Bone Arch*, The famous *Magpie Café* for the best fish and chips in Whitby, *the harbour*, *the beach, the views...* I could go on and on, but one thing was for sure, I could never swap that for a life in the city – who would?!

I had taken the train to Leeds for our first date, and Eric had met me at the station – it had been a lovely sunny day in July, and I had been wearing a blue floaty summer dress with silver sandals, Eric, however, all six foot three of him, was still in a suit – and I had laughed, he definitely was a city boy through and through.

The restaurant that he had taken me to was beautiful, and a million miles out of my league. I remember that I had felt awkward and totally out of place, praying for the time to pass by quickly so that I could get back on the train and go home.

It wasn't that Eric was poor company, or that we had nothing to talk about, but I was more of a greasy spoon kind of girl, not a *try and work out which cutlery is for what* kind of girl – and I had blushed furiously when I had used the wrong knife and fork for our starter – Eric though had chuckled, only commenting that he was getting *Pretty Woman* vibes from our date, and I hadn't exactly known how to take that comment – considering that *Julia Roberts* was a hooker in that movie. I had however laughed it off and picked up the menu, wondering to myself if it would be improper to dive into the breadbasket while we waited to order.

'The menu looks delicious! What will you have do you think?' I had asked, wide-eyed and trying to contain my hunger pangs – everything had sounded wonderful, and I had wanted to try them all.

Yep, I was one of those lucky girls with a huge appetite and fast metabolism, so I had never had to worry about my figure, after all a girl must eat.

'The lobster of course, and you? What will you have?'

'Oh, I don't know, the carbonara maybe, with fries and deep-fried mushrooms in three cheese sauce.' I smiled, 'and definitely the death by chocolate cake to finish!'

I hadn't missed his raised eyebrow, I hadn't missed the way that he had looked down his nose at me, but I had ignored it – I had purposely ignored it!

'Oh, wow! That's, *wow, a lot!* – are you sure you want to ruin that amazing figure for cheesy mushrooms?'

I laughed, uneasily, and picked up the menu once more, not wanting to ruin our perfect first date by arguing over mushrooms, 'I'm joking of course. Obviously, I will take the caesar salad, it sounds… delicious.'

He had visibly relaxed, 'Excellent. The salad it is. I knew you would make the right choice.'

'Yeah.' I had mumbled, 'I guess I just needed reminding.'

'Oh that's okay, I can keep you on track.' He had winked, smiling up at the waiter who was taking our order.

Why did I stay?

Why didn't I just pick up my handbag and leave?

Was I that desperate to connect with somebody? To have a man take interest in me? I had sworn off men, I had been content in that decision, so why then would I put up with such churlish behaviour from a man that I had no real emotional connection with?

Because I'd had my head turned by the handsome businessman, that's why. And like a love-struck teenager who didn't know any better, I had laughed the insults off.

Yet another decision that I would live to regret.

Once our meal was over Eric had taken me to see the sights, *The Art Gallery*, *Town Hall*, *Civic Centre*, *Leeds City Museum*, *The Royal Armouries* and *Kirkgate Market*. They were lovely of course but extremely busy, and I knew as I always had, that I would never swap my life in Whitby for a city as bustling as Leeds.

After refusing Eric's offer of staying overnight at his apartment, I boarded my train unsure of whether or not I would see him again.

The date had been fine, but there had been something - other than the not-so-veiled insults that just wouldn't stop nagging away at the back of my mind, something that I couldn't quite put my finger on.

Why would a man like Eric be interested in a woman like me? He was successful, not socially awkward, presentable, financially stable, and confident.

What was I?

A shop assistant with average confidence and average social skills. The only reason I owned my house was because of the inheritance money that I received when my grandmother passed – a substantial amount that had permitted me the luxury of purchasing my home outright and still left me with more than a comfortable bank balance. And what a perfect home it was, overlooking the harbour. From my balcony, I had the most spectacular views of the North Sea, the beaches and the pier. – but had that really been enough to turn Eric's head? Had it?

Eric didn't know about my money – not that he needed extra cash of course – but I didn't want to blow it on nights out and holidays with a new man – I wanted to save it – for one of those random rainy days. So it wasn't money that attracted him to me.

Sure, I was pretty and slim – but was that really enough for a man like him? A man that could surely have any woman that he wanted.

A man that no doubt had already had as many women as he wanted.

As the train had happily rumbled along the tracks I had only one question left on my mind - was I really prepared to give up my quiet, single life for the hectic city life of Eric Sawyer?

Despite my reservations, I agreed to go on a second date with Eric, and it had, to my surprise been wonderful. We had spent a lovely day in Scarborough, walking along the beach, eating ice-cream, spending two pence pieces in the arcades and eating fish and chips. I couldn't have wished for better company and saw almost immediately that Eric from the pub was long gone, and so I had put his terrible behaviour down to tiredness and stress at work, relieved that I was wrong about him.

Our third date however did throw up a few concerns, which I again brushed to one side. We had made reservations for a lovely restaurant in Leeds, and as we had waited for our meal, we had chatted pleasantly, laughing and smiling at everything, as you do in a very new, very fresh romance. But when Eric's food arrived that smiling face had darkened, as he noticed instantly that his steak was overcooked. I had cringed with embarrassment as he had torn a strip off of the poor waitress, and no matter how hard I tried to calm him down he just would not let it go, he certainly seemed intent on humiliating the poor girl.

No matter how many times she apologised, no matter her tears, Eric was totally unmoved. I did at one point apologise on his behalf but received such a scathing glare from him that I instantly shrank back into my chair, deciding it would be best not to speak again.

Unfortunately, the foul atmosphere from the restaurant followed us around for the remainder of our date, with Eric brooding and snapping at people for no obvious reason, my discomfort plain to see, and at other times ignoring me completely, despite my efforts to engage him in any kind of conversation. As far as I was concerned, he had ruined the entire day with his appalling attitude, and I was glad when it was once again time to board the train home. He had called me later that evening to apologise, and while I was still a little miffed with him, I did in the end, stupidly, accept his apology. He told me that he thought he was coming down with something, that he was tired, and that he was always a grumpy sod when he was tired or unwell, and I believed him.

Over the months that followed, I began to see more and more of Eric, much to the detriment of my relationship with Heidi and the girls, but as Eric had said, our relationship was new and we were still in the stages of getting to know each other, whereas I already knew all I needed to know about my best friends, which at the time had seemed to make a lot of sense to me, and I had happily agreed with him.

We had lazy days on the beach, just the two of us, away in a world of our own – we did not let anybody in, Eric preferred it that way – no distractions, no interruptions. Eric preferred that we didn't take our mobile phones with us on our little breaks away together, that way he could ensure that we weren't preoccupied with text messages and emails – though I am sure that I heard his phone vibrate somewhere deep inside his suitcase on more than one occasion. I hadn't questioned it though, as I knew what a workaholic he was – but still, it had hardly seemed fair.

We had cosy nights in, watching movies and reading books, day trips to other seaside towns and weekend breaks in the Yorkshire Dales. It was pure bliss.

Sure, we had our spats like any other couple, and I had found it easier to back down than let the argument fester and ruin our time together. After all, all couples argued.

Eric could be so warm, so loving - as close to perfect as you could get. But then like a light being switched off, he would change. Become moody, sullen, and bad-tempered – and no matter what I did, it would always be wrong.

In those moments, I thought about ending things, I thought about giving him up – but then he would travel over after work with flowers, chocolates and a movie, he would run me a hot bath and massage my feet, and I would tell myself that everything would be fine now.

I would tell myself that it was my fault, that I was the one causing these problems, and that I needed to fix myself.

I hadn't seen the warning signs, or maybe in truth I had, and I had refused to believe them – but how could I have known the difference between love and domination when he treated me like a princess for the most part?

When the sarcastic remarks and predatory actions were so subtle that I believed constantly that I had imagined them?

On the days that Eric could not make it across to me, I would have fun with the girls, drinking until our inhibitions were totally gone, and laughing until our bellies ached, though that all stopped when Eric reappeared, and I would not see my friends again until he had gone back home. I felt free on those days, and yet I still counted down the hours until I could see him again.

One chilly November Thursday however, I had texted Eric to let him know that I would not be able to see him at the weekend as previously arranged, as I had made plans to meet Heidi, Nicky and Jessica in *The Dirty Rabbit* for an early lunch on Saturday and then go Christmas shopping, we would then be having a present wrapping day on Sunday, but that I looked forward to seeing him the following weekend.

He had not responded.

Putting it down to him being busy with work, and that I would no doubt hear from him later, I had set out on that

Saturday afternoon to meet the girls as arranged, only to bump into Eric outside of the bar.

Shocked to see him, as I had already made him aware that I was not available, I mumbled a slightly irritated hello and asked him what he was doing here, and hadn't he received my message?

He had simply shrugged and said that he thought he would join us, that way we could kill two birds with one stone.

Biting down my frustration, I pushed open the doors of the bar and tried my best to ignore the flash of anger upon Heidi's face.

I suppose that I should have ended things there and then, I should have put my friends first, but Eric was being his usual charming self, and before I knew it, I had forgotten all about my earlier frustration with him, and as we had shopped for presents, I had felt warm and fuzzy inside – knowing that I had against all odds fallen head over heels in love with the man.

I know that some of the things that Eric did for me, for us, frustrated Heidi, but she just didn't see him as I did. She didn't see how caring and considerate he was of me, how his every thought every single day was of me, and only me.

He would call me first thing in the morning and last

thing at night, always on my landline to make sure that I was at home, safe.

He even suggested downloading a tracker app onto my mobile phone so that he could see that I had made it home okay if I was working the late shift.

He would offer to pick me up from nights out with my friends, even if that did mean that more often than not, I had to leave earlier than them, but I didn't grumble, because I knew that he had travelled from Leeds especially to do this for me.

I had explained all of this to Heidi, but she had remained unmoved by him, and I suppose our friendship was fractured from that moment on.

But I would not give him up - not for anyone.

It came as a complete surprise to me when after only twelve months Eric suggested that we move in together.

I had panicked as I knew that I absolutely did not want to leave Whitby, and I certainly did not want to move to Leeds – but he had said with a smile that he would move in with me, and I had panicked again, knowing that my safe haven would now be a shared space and that seeing the girls would definitely be harder once he moved in.

But he had smiled that ever so charming and disarming

smile, and I had known that everything would work out just fine.

I knew that once we were seeing each other seven days a week, and the honeymoon period was over, we would each see our friends as often as we liked.

Heidi had expressed major concerns, even going as far as to stage an intervention in *The Dirty Rabbit*, but I had managed to convince the girls that I was happy, and couldn't they too be happy for me?

It didn't take long for Eric to relocate his business, as the majority of it was run virtually any way.

He had decided to keep his apartment, as he said it would come in handy for when he had late-night client meetings. I had agreed, even though deep down I felt somewhat confused.

Before I knew it, he was sharing my bed every night, waking me up with kisses and breakfast, and any fears that I may have harboured that he would be untidy had been quickly quashed, as Eric, it would seem, was incredibly OCD about certain things, and had some rather peculiar idiosyncrasies.

For example, Eric must always, and I mean always, close the vertical blinds to the left, cups must be arranged in the cupboard with their handles to the right, and his clothes, and now mine it would seem, must be hung in colour order - all white together, all black together etc.

Tins of food must be lined up perfectly, alphabetically and by content, and cushions must be sat perfectly square and not in a diamond shape as I preferred.

I was shocked the first time I had seen his wardrobe layout, and I laughed at how regimented it had seemed, but when I discovered the cupboards and the cups, I questioned him.

'Why?' I had laughed, 'Why is this *a thing*?'

'What do you mean, *why?*' he had answered quietly, so quietly in fact that I almost hadn't heard him.

Laughing again, I opened the cupboard door and pointed out the tins, 'why are you arranging the tins like this? Don't you think it's a little bit, well, odd?'

'You think I'm odd?'

'No. I don't think *you* are odd; I just think *this* is odd. And don't even get me started on the wardrobes.'

'You have a problem with the way that I arrange things? I would have thought all women would prefer a tidy man. But then I suppose that you aren't really like all women, are you, Jade!'

'What do you mean?' I had asked, shocked by the sudden change in him, 'I think that I am perfectly fine the way that

I am, thank you very much'

'Oh, do you?! And what makes you so perfect, eh Jade?'

'I never said that I was perfect. I said that I was perfectly fine with how I am. What the hell is wrong with you? You know...' I sighed, '...if you don't think I'm good enough for you, you can always leave.'

'Oh, you'd like that, wouldn't you?! I gave up everything for you, what have you given up for me?'

Shocked, I had leant back against the kitchen worktop, my chest heaving with the force of his accusations, and this overwhelming and unexpected attack. 'I gave up my life for you!' I snapped back. 'My friends, my freedom, everything! I'm only twenty-eight for crying out loud and I have nothing! You couldn't even sell your apartment, and we both know why that is don't we!'

I couldn't understand where my words had come from – had I secretly been harbouring these thoughts about Eric? 'Oh boo hoo! I'm twenty-eight too Jade and I have my own business, so whose fault is it that you have nothing! You know damn well why I kept the apartment on, so if you know something that I don't, please do enlighten me!'

'You really need me to spell it out?'

'I think I do, yeah.'

'You have the apartment so that you can see other women,

I'm not stupid Eric, I know what you do there.'

'Oh? And what do I do there?' He had mocked.

'You…' I faltered, not wanting to say the words that once spoken could never be taken back. 'You…'

'Have sex? Is that it Jade? What, you can't say the word? Sex Jade. Sex, sex, sex!'

'You pig!' I had spit, 'you disgusting pig!'

'So what if I do Jade? Maybe I need something a little less *vanilla* sometimes!'

'So why did you choose me? Why did you, bigshot, Eric bloody Sawyer choose poor pathetic little Jade Locke? Why Eric? Why?'

'Maybe I felt sorry for you!' he snarled, 'You want your friends and your freedom Jade? Then go, go to them, go to them right now!' he had snarled, 'But I won't be here when you get back. Is that what you want?'

'I just wanted to know why you arrange the tins this way?!' I screamed, pulling them maniacally from the cupboards and launching them across the kitchen. 'Why?! Why can't you ever give me a straight answer? Why do you always blame me? They're just tins, Eric! Why are you being like this?'

He had towered over me then, all six foot three of him – his wide shoulders blocking everything from view, as his face had leant closely into mine.

I tried to keep eye contact with him, I tried not to back down – but his eyes were dead, like a shark's eyes, and I could not help but look away.

'Because this is how *I* want it, Jade. This is how *we* will be doing things from now on, so I suggest…' he had tapped my forehead hard with his finger, '…that you try and get it into your thick skull!'

'Look.' I had snapped back while pushing his hand away from my face, 'if you want to arrange your clothes by bloody shade of green, or whatever, then you do so, but I won't be!'

He had raised his hand to me then.

He didn't strike me, he didn't do anything - but the intention had been clear, and I had nodded meekly, my fear of him at that moment evident upon my face, and I agreed that maybe it was a good idea to get organised.

I know, I know, the warning sign was practically fifty feet tall in neon lights, but I ignored it. I wanted to ignore it. I knowingly turned the proverbial blind eye.

I didn't want anything to ruin our love.

Not even a raised hand or him cheating on me.

I just wanted to have a peaceful loving relationship with the man that I loved.

I didn't want arguments and screaming and name-calling. The mood changes and the sarcastic comments.

I wanted the fairy-tale.

Didn't I deserve the fairy-tale?

I would not give up on Eric. I would not give up on us. Surely the good more than outweighed the bad?

He had apologised afterwards and kissed my forehead, telling me that I shouldn't have pushed his buttons, that I knew how crazy it made him.

He said together we can *'work on you'* – I didn't know what that meant, but I nodded my head and agreed anyway.

So, I soon learnt how to close the blinds properly, arrange the pillows and put away the cups and tins, and eventually, it became second nature, just as he said it would.

Eric was so pleased with me, and in turn, our relationship flourished.

I knew then that the best way to keep things peaceful was to just do as he wanted.

Weeks had passed since the kitchen fiasco without further incident, and so I had asked somewhat cautiously if Eric would like to meet my parents – he had appeared overjoyed at the suggestion, so I had promptly made arrangements to pay them a long overdue visit.

It was only a twenty-minute drive to my mum and dad's place in Robin Hoods Bay, and I knew that there was no way we could fall out again on such a short journey.

For that, I had been thankful.

My parents, George and Evelyn, both in their sixties, as predicted absolutely loved Eric, declaring happily that they were pleased to see me finally settled.

Dad embarrassingly had commented on the size of Eric's muscles – requesting to know how he became so well built and did he have any tips. Mum had laughed, knowing as well as I did that dad had no intention of ever hitting the gym. The nearest thing that dad did to actual exercise was dead heading mum's roses - (*tentatively I must add*).

Mum had always had a green finger, something that I had never acquired, and her garden was the envy of the small fishing village where they lived. Her roses had even won prizes, they were that fabulous!

'You look wonderful.' Mum had whispered out of earshot of the men while admiring my blue summer dress, 'it must be love.'

'I think you might be right.' I giggled. 'He's just so… oh I don't know mum, just so.'

'Just so blooming handsome.' She had laughed, taking my hand and steering me towards the overflowing dining table, 'you keep both hands tightly on this one. He's a keeper.'

'I think I may have gotten it right this time mum, I think I finally hit the jackpot.'

'Well after *he who shall not be named,* you deserve to be happy! I'm sorry you had to go through that. Heartbreak really is the worst.'

'I did love him.' I had shrugged, 'but it just wasn't meant to be. I guess Cupid had other ideas for me.'

I hadn't told mum my concerns about Eric raising his hand to me, I didn't want her to worry, or to say something that could never be unsaid, and really – I did start it.

'I think you might be right – for once stupid Cupid got it spot on.'

After the delicious dinner that mum had lovingly prepared – (*roast beef with all of the trimmings*), we headed out into the aforementioned prize-winning garden to soak up the last of the day's sunshine. It was then that mum had asked if I had met Eric's parents yet.

It wasn't a subject that Eric and I had yet discussed, and despite my eagerness to meet his parents I had not dared bring it up. I cannot say why, I just felt like it was something that Eric would arrange when he was ready.

'Ah.' Eric had mumbled sadly, 'That may be a bit of a problem – my parents are no longer with us I'm afraid.' I had been shocked that I was only just hearing about this now when Eric had ample opportunity to tell me in private.

'Oh, my god.' My mum gasped, 'what happened? If you don't mind my asking.' She had quickly added.

'No, not at all.' He smiled, warmly, 'it was a boating accident. I was just a kid, so I don't remember too much myself. I think my father had a little too much liquid confidence in himself, and not nearly enough knowledge of boats. He crashed the boat, and mum and dad drowned, but I somehow didn't. I can't really remember much about it.'

'Was your father a big drinker then?' Dad asked, shocked.

'Oh yeah. Once he was on a bender there was no stopping him – that's why I'm surprised mum allowed me to even go with them – she knew what he was like.'

'Was your mum scared of him?' My mum had asked, sadly.

'Oh yeah. My dad was a bully of a man – took his belt to me more than once for absolutely nothing. Makes you think though doesn't it…'

'What's that?' Dad had asked.

'Why some people are so weak? If she'd just been a stronger person, then she'd still be alive.'

'Well, fear does funny things to you.' Soothed mum, 'I'm sure she wanted to.'

'But she didn't, did she!' He had growled. 'She didn't!'

'My god Eric, why didn't you tell me?' I had asked, completely overwhelmed and embarrassed, 'I'm so sorry – I wish that I had known.'

'Why? It's not like you killed them.' He had laughed solemnly, as we had all fallen silent.

'Well, I have to say that you have certainly made something of yourself out of this tragedy.' Dad had smiled, nervously patting Eric on the back and breaking the awkward silence that had descended.

'Thank you, George.' He had grinned, 'I like to think so.'

As the afternoon had passed peacefully, and without any further shocking declarations, I had pondered why Eric would choose now to tell me his parents were dead? Surely, he would know that my parents would ask?

Was he trying to humiliate me?

Trying to prove a point that I didn't know everything about him as I assumed that I did?

I had waited until we had said our goodbyes and were settled back in the car before I decided to broach the subject with him.

My questioning of Eric hadn't gone well at all, and despite it being many years ago now, I remember it as clearly as if it had only just occurred.

I remember taking a deep breath and pushing a loose strand of hair behind my ear as I turned to face Eric. He looked so deep in thought, and I had known that my interrupting him wouldn't go down so well, but I needed answers. He owed me answers.

'Eric…' I had begun, shakily, 'what was all of that back there? I don't understand.'

'What do you need to understand about it?' he answered, not looking at me.

'Well, Eric… I mean c'mon, you just drop out of the blue that your parents are deceased? You didn't think that was something that I should have been made aware of?'

'What's the problem here?' he snarled, finally turning to look at me, his eyes wild, 'they're not your parents.'

'I just thought that maybe you would share something like that with me. I….'

'This is just typical of you Jade, always making everything about you! Just bloody typical!'

'Eric, no! That isn't what's happening here. I just would

44

have preferred it if you'd told me beforehand that's all.'

'You know now, so what's the big deal?'

'It isn't a big deal!' I had snapped, completely frustrated that he wouldn't give me a straight answer, 'I just would have thought...'

'Jade, I'm driving here for crying out loud! I need to concentrate!'

'Concentrate?! You are driving thirty-two miles per hour, what the hell could you possibly need to concentrate on!'

'Do you want to drive?' he had growled, 'or maybe you'd prefer to walk?' Slamming on the breaks he had reached across me and pushed open my door with a grunt of frustration, 'go on, get out!'

'Eric...I...'

'Out!' he had shouted, as I frantically grabbed my handbag and scrambled from the car, 'we talk when I say!'

'Eric, please, don't do this.' I had pleaded pointlessly as he slammed the door shut and sped away from me, 'ERIC!' I had screamed after the retreating car, sure that he would calm down and return to pick me up. Apologetic, eager to make it up to me.

But he did not return.

He had abandoned me.

The walk itself would have been semi-pleasant, had I not

been wearing strappy sandals, and if I had thought to grab my jacket from the backseat of the car. But with each minute that passed of my near on five-mile walk, I had winced at the burning pain in my feet, knowing that blisters would be forming, and I had shivered against the chill wind that was blowing in from the North Sea.

I could have called any of the girls to come and pick me up, or my mum and dad - they would have dropped everything in an instant, but I couldn't form a story believable enough in my mind that would explain my current predicament. They would have seen right through me anyway, and I honestly could not have faced the humiliation.

I couldn't call a taxi as I had no money on me and not enough signal strength to use the taxi app on my phone. So, it was walking or staying rooted to the spot.

Did I really mean so little to him?

But he wasn't to blame, I knew that he wasn't.

Did I really need to bring up his dead parents, *again?*

Was it even that important that he didn't tell me?

Was it all over between us now?

Not even for a moment did I consider that it was *his* behaviour that was appalling, that *he* was the one in the wrong.

No.

I had blamed myself, and once home, exhausted from walking and exhausted from crying, I had been the one to apologise - but not once did the word *sorry* pass *his* lips.

Eric's marriage proposal some six months later came as a complete surprise to me, as our relationship had been somewhat up and down since the *car incident*.
We had had some wonderful moments since then too, don't get me wrong, but I hadn't even entertained the notion that marriage was on the cards.

I had thought, glumly, that we would eventfully just fizzle out, once Eric was bored of fighting with me – once he realised that he could be with a woman that didn't push his buttons.

I had been wrong.
But I seemed to have been wrong about a lot of things back then.

On the day of the proposal, Eric had asked me to meet him at the *Whale Bone Arch* at exactly four P.M – he didn't say why, he just said that I could not be late, and I could not be early, it had to be dead on four P.M.

Knowing Eric as I did then, I knew that he would not be pleased if I disregarded his instructions, and I couldn't bear the thought of us falling out *again*.

I had wrapped up warm, it was the middle of December after all, and knowing that it was only really a fifteen-minute walk, I had set off with plenty of time to spare – I wouldn't of course arrive early, I had planned instead to hide out by the *Royal Hotel* until there were only thirty seconds or so left until the rendezvous time.

I couldn't think for the life of me why Eric would want to meet me outside in the cold when we could have met at *The Dirty Rabbit* – but then Eric didn't often do things that made sense to anyone else.

When the time had arrived, I made sure to jump up and down on the spot a few times, so that Eric wouldn't be suspicious as to why I wasn't out of breath from walking, and I had made my way across to the *Whale Bone Arch*, all the while keeping a watchful eye on the time.

I didn't immediately see him when I arrived, and I felt a little relieved – maybe he had forgotten. But I knew that Eric never forgot anything, not unless it suited him to do so.

'Jade!' he had exclaimed, excitedly, almost appearing as if by magic, as he pulled me into a tight and slightly uncomfortable embrace. 'You made it, and…' he glanced at his watch, 'right on time too.'

'Well, you did say four, so I…'

'I did, and you didn't disappoint.' He had grinned, looking around himself, almost nervously.

'What's all this about?' I had asked, pulling myself out of his arms, 'what's going on?'

'You'll see, you'll see.'

Now I can't quite explain the feeling that shot through me as Eric dropped down to one knee and produced a ring, nor can I explain the feeling of seeing all of my friends, Heidi, Nicky, Jessica, a few friendly locals from the bar, Mary from the corner shop, (*Gordon couldn't make it as he was working*) - suddenly surrounding me, but I can describe how I felt when I looked at Heidi – because unlike the others she was not smiling, she looked concerned.

I had felt hurt then; heart-shattering hurt – why couldn't she just be happy for me? Just because she had suffered badly at the hands of her ex-partner didn't mean that all men were *that* man.

I knew that it was a dreadful thing to think, I knew that it wasn't even remotely the same thing, but still, the thought entered my mind and I resented her for it.

'Well?' Eric had prompted, as I realised in horror that I had missed his entire proposal speech, 'What's it going to be?'

I had nodded slowly and then avoiding eye contact with Heidi I had screamed 'Yes!', Eric had smiled up at me then and slipped a beautiful solitaire diamond ring onto my finger. I was to be married! And yet all I cared about at that moment was the look on Heidi's face.

After much cooing over my engagement ring, we had all decided that it was much too cold to be standing around outside and had headed instead to *The Dirty Rabbit* for an impromptu engagement party.

Once there, I pulled Heidi to one side in the ladies and asked her why she looked so sad, was she not happy for me? And she had said that she was, but she didn't want to see me making the same mistakes that she had.

I couldn't immediately respond, she was my best friend, but maybe she didn't know me quite as well as she thought she did. I had reassured her eventually that I was happy, that Eric was everything that I wanted, and that she would be the first one to know if I was not.

She had nodded, knowing as I did that it was a blatant lie. I would never admit that I was wrong about him because we both knew that I didn't want to be wrong about him.

I just wanted to be happy. I didn't want the heartache again that I had felt with Damon, I just wanted to be loved – and if that meant putting up with Eric's sometimes *off-the-wall* behaviour, then so be it.

We had had so many wonderful times together since our first meeting, but I knew, even then that I thought those thoughts intentionally, to convince myself I suppose, that Eric was perfect – that Eric was nothing like Damon – that I had finally found my prince charming – albeit a slightly untraditional, unstable one.

But I would make it work this time. I would.

Leaving Heidi to fix her makeup, I pushed my way through the now-crowded room and headed immediately to the bar – where Eric was buying drinks for everybody that wished to celebrate with us.

He was in high spirits, telling jokes, talking about football – despite having no interest in the sport whatsoever, singing tunelessly to the jukebox and generally being a wonderful host. I had felt content – for the first time since he proposed I had felt pure and blissful contentment.

The hours seemed to fly by, as I flitted from one table to the next, accepting congratulations and well wishes from friends and strangers alike, both of whom were insistent on buying me drinks – I had felt as free as a bird, and as I had raised my glass to cheer our upcoming nuptials, I had almost instantly felt it being removed from my hand.

'Don't you think that maybe you've had enough?' Eric had whispered into my ear. 'Maybe have some water.'

Stunned I turned to face him, 'Water?' I laughed, 'it's a party! Who drinks water at a party? Pass me my drink please.'

'Water Jade!' he had growled, 'no more alcohol for you. You are embarrassing yourself, and you are embarrassing me!'

'How exactly am I embarrassing you?' I chuckled, 'I'm just having fun – you remember fun, right?'

'Is that what you call flirting with every man in the place? *Fun*? You really do have a warped idea of Fun.' He had snarled, his eyes bulging with rage,

'Flirting with every… Now you listen here…'

'Just order the damn water, Jade!'

'Are you crazy?' I had asked, reaching across him to get at my drink, 'I'll drink what the hell I like.'

Feeling his fingers digging roughly into my arm I backed away from the drink that he had taken from me and smiled politely at the barman instead. 'Could I get another double Vodka and Coke, please? My fiancé has decided that he wants to drink mine.'

'Ah well.' He had laughed, 'he is the man of the house now.'

'Yeah right.' I muttered under my breath, while still smiling sweetly at him as he passed across my new glass.

Leaning into me, Eric had made a show of gently kissing my cheek, but what nobody saw or heard was the veiled threat that he had made if I so much as took one sip. Losing my bravado, I had shakily placed my glass back onto the bar and asked the barman for water instead, with the excuse that I was suddenly feeling a little unwell.

'Unwell?' Heidi had laughed from behind me, 'since when were you such a lightweight? You could drink everybody in here under the table.'

She was right, I could handle my alcohol, but was it really worth fighting with Eric over?

'I think maybe it's just the day catching up with me.' I had mumbled, with a theatrical yawn, 'I might just call it a night actually, I'm so tired.'

'Like hell you will!' She had laughed, reaching across Eric to get at my original drink, 'get this down you! A few more of these and you'll be up dancing like a lunatic and taking over the karaoke machine! Go home, as if!'

'She said...' Eric growled, menacingly, removing the glass once more, '...that she doesn't want it!'

'Well, I don't think that you're her keeper, so pass it back and let the girl celebrate.'

'We're done celebrating!' He had snapped back, daring Heidi to speak even one more word – but he didn't know Heidi as I did.

'On your terms only, is it?' she had asked, 'what Jade can and can't do?'

'Heidi, please.' I had begged, 'Just leave it.'

'I won't leave it! He's controlling you; can't you see that?'

'It's just one drink, and I really don't feel well.'

'*He* makes you unwell.' She had spit, '*he* is doing this to you.'

'Heidi he isn't! It's all in your head!'

'Oh? Is that how you think of me? I get into one bad relationship and now I think every man is a psycho?' She sounded hurt, and I felt terrible, but I could not let this blow up any more than it already had.

'That isn't what I meant at all. It's just, you do seem to have a lot of issues with Eric and you barely even know him. I'm stuck here Heidi, right in the middle.'

'He has you stuck that's why.' She had argued, prodding Eric with a manicured fingernail. 'He has you stuck because it's easier for him, it makes him feel like the big man! You don't have to stay Jade, you don't.'

'Heidi please.' I had begged, 'please just try, for me.'

'I can't. I know this type of man Jade, him taking your drink is just the beginning.'

'Heidi...'

Eric remained silent until the point that people started to look over at us, and I knew that he would not allow anybody to make a show of him.

'Well.' He hollered, 'Jade here has celebrated a little too hard.' The bar had erupted into whoops and cheers, 'I reckon I should take her home and put her to bed.' More whoops and cheers ensued, all of which drowned out Heidi's protests. 'Thank you all for celebrating with us today.' He had raised his glass, 'here's to the big day!'

We had left in a hurry after that, with much back-slapping and cheek-kissing along the way, and I had known that once outside I would no longer be safe.

But Eric had done nothing – he had not acted upon his earlier threat – he had as promised tucked me up in bed, kissed my forehead and brought me a glass of water. His only parting words before turning off the light had been that Heidi would no longer be welcome at our wedding.

Five months had passed before Heidi and I had spoken again. I hadn't intentionally avoided her; I just didn't seem to have time for anything as I once had.

I hadn't been to *The Dirty Rabbit* in months either, so had not had any kind of catch-up with Nicky or Jessica – it had felt like my life was no longer my own.

In-between Eric and my new job there just didn't seem to be enough hours in the day. But Heidi and I had bumped into each other outside of the supermarket one sunny day in May, and at that point, it was near on impossible not to acknowledge one another's presence.

It had been awkward, not knowing how to start a conversation after what had happened back in December, and it had been sad to know that the person I had known for years was now like a stranger.

'Heidi.' I had begun slowly, 'Can I apologise for my behaviour in the bar? I am so sorry. I…'

'Your behaviour?!' She had snapped, 'don't you mean…' She stopped when she saw the look on my face and tried a different approach. 'Look, Jade, I'm never going to be Eric's number one fan, I'm just not – because I don't think that he's right for you. But I have to trust that you know what you're doing and that if you ever, and I do mean ever, need to get away from him…'

'I won't need to Heidi. I promise you that I won't. Can we just call a truce? Please?'

She paused, and then smiled, pulling me into her arms, 'I've missed you so much.' She had sobbed against my neck, 'I don't ever want us to fall out again, okay?'

Sobbing myself I had promised her *(a promise that I would later break)* that we would never be apart again, ever!

I hadn't told her what Eric had said about the wedding, as I knew, or rather hoped, that I could work on him and get him to change his mind – I also knew at that moment that he could not find out about our renewed friendship, not until I was ready to tell him.

And so, I met Heidi in secret. She didn't know it was a secret and I didn't tell her it was, though I think she suspected something was going on.

I would use holiday days from work to meet her, say I was working the late shift, or that I had to cover a shift for another worker – thankful now that I had never let Eric install that stupid tracker on my phone.

I know that I shouldn't have lied to him, but it was the only thing at that time that I could say was all mine. And I needed my best friend, I really needed her.

Regarding my upcoming wedding, Heidi agreed to help

and somewhat reluctantly tagged along as I chose my wedding dress.

Nicky and Jessica took care of the hairdresser and the makeup artist, while Eric and I planned together the venue and the honeymoon.

Our wedding was to take place at the *Royal Hotel*, which was situated just across from the *Whale Bone Arch*, the setting of my rather haphazard proposal, but putting that aside, the views were spectacular as it was situated in the west cliff area of Whitby.

I had wanted pale pink chairs and table covers, but Eric had thought that was tacky and in front of the wedding organiser had shot me down, instead demanding that we go with plain white chairs and covers and simple silverware.

I had felt humiliated.

I had said nothing.

I don't know how it all came together, but somehow in the space of a few short months, we had planned the entire wedding, well Eric had, but my one small victory was that I had managed to convince him to let Heidi attend after all. He hadn't wanted to back down, but after I explained how odd it would look if my best friend wasn't there on the biggest day of my life, he had done just that.

Eric was all about saving face.
His own anyway.

On the day of my wedding, I felt ill.

Despite it being a hot August afternoon, I felt a chill in my bones. I had felt like I couldn't go through with it – that something was just *off*. But I had convinced myself, as I did so many times back then, that it was just wedding day jitters, and that once I had my gown on and the music began to play everything would be perfect.

But despite the clever way that I had talked myself around, the butterflies were still there, fluttering lightly in my stomach, gently letting me know that there was still time to back out.

I had expected Heidi to try just one more time to put an end to this charade, to tell me that I was stupid, that he didn't love me, that he was all wrong for me. But she hadn't.

She had just smiled as she helped me into my wedding dress and told me that I looked beautiful.

Would I have walked away from Eric if she had tried one more time?

Would I finally have accepted that she was right, that the nagging thoughts in my head were right?

I wish even now that I could say yes, that I could blame somebody else for my mistake, for what was to come – but that would be wrong, and it would be unfair.

It was not Heidi's job to save me.

Eric had chosen *By the light of the silvery moon* as the song that I would walk down the aisle to, as it was the song that was playing when we first met. It wasn't what I would have chosen, but he was adamant, and I saw no point in us falling out over a stupid song.

My gown was ivory lace, simple yet elegant, and my bridesmaids, Heidi, Jessica and Nicky wore pale pink floor-length dresses. Eric hadn't wanted Heidi to be a bridesmaid, but again I had convinced him otherwise – explaining that people would wonder why she wasn't part of the bridal party – and that I didn't want those questions to ruin our big day. He had again reluctantly agreed.

As my dad had walked me down the aisle towards Eric, who had looked perfect in his tailor-made suit, his bright white teeth gleaming and not a hair out of place on his handsome head, the gentle flutter of the butterfly wings had become stronger, almost deafening, and I had paused, just for the briefest of moments to catch my breath. Nobody seemed to have noticed my momentary hesitation, but Eric had, and the flash of darkness that spread across his face had spoken volumes to me.

'You alright love?' Dad had asked, looking at me with concern in his eyes, the grip of his hand on my arm becoming just a little tighter.

I hadn't been able to answer.

I knew that my voice would give me away in seconds, so I smiled, nodded my head, and put all of my concentration into getting to the end of the aisle without breaking down.

I just wanted it to be over.

The pressure was too much.

Why didn't I just turn and run? Nobody would have stopped me, they'd have all been too shocked to move – but Heidi would have followed, she'd have had my back – but I didn't run. I just smiled up at my husband-to-be and prayed for the butterflies to be silent.

My mum, wiping tears from her eyes had mouthed to me that I looked beautiful, while my dad held onto me for dear life, almost as though he wasn't quite ready to hand his daughter over – like the years had passed way too quickly for him to comprehend, and as he had removed his arm from mine, I had felt overwhelming emptiness consume me – this was really happening – this was really my life now.

I felt sick.

The ceremony had passed in a blur, I couldn't remember speaking my vows, I couldn't remember exchanging rings, I couldn't remember kissing the groom – but all of a sudden, we were married – all of a sudden, we were husband and wife, and everybody was cheering and throwing confetti over our heads.

I was married.

I was now Mrs Sawyer.

So why then, on the happiest day of my life, did I feel so sad?

The wedding party was in full swing as Eric and I had made our grand entrance as Mr and Mrs Sawyer, and as he had spun me around the dancefloor to *Elvis Presley's, Can't help falling in love* – again, not my choice, I had wanted nothing more than to sit down and just have five minutes to myself.

Heidi, Jessica, Nicky and Gordon, were having a ball on the dancefloor – though how they were even able to move after the three-course meal that had been served only hours before was beyond my comprehension. I had felt suffocated in my gown, and it seemed to become tighter with each hour that passed. I could understand, as I had wiggled uncomfortably, why some brides chose another outfit for the reception.

Other than one dance with my dad, and a brief hug and chat with my mum, I had spent the rest of the evening glued to Eric's side, reluctantly posing for photographs, cutting the wedding cake, smiling on command, laughing at jokes that I didn't understand, and making polite small talk with relatives that I had no recollection of ever meeting before the wedding, and by midnight I was exhausted. All I wanted to do was peel myself out of my wedding dress, kick off my heels and sleep – but Eric had other ideas.

As Eric had stumbled into our honeymoon suite, I had hoped that he would be much too drunk to want to consummate our marriage, but he had awkwardly lunged towards me, all but ripping the buttons on the back of my dress in his desperation to get me out of it. I had gently pushed him away; told him I was too tired and that it had been a long day – surely, he just wanted to sleep too?
His anger had been quick to surface, as my now torn dress fell to the floor in a tattered heap.
'Too tired little baby.' He had mocked, as I tried to cover myself with my hands. My bridal lingerie was beautiful

and expensive, but it suddenly felt cheap and vulgar with his eyes upon it.

'It's just been a long day Eric...' I protested as he reached out again, '...let's just get some sleep, okay?'

'I don't want sleep, *Mrs Sawyer.*' He had hissed, 'I want what is my right!'

'Eric, no!' I had snapped back, afraid and sapped of all energy, 'You are drunk, and I am drained, let's just talk in the morning, I...'

His hands had been around my throat then, and as I had struggled, he had forced me back onto the bed, the full weight of him crushing my body. At six foot three and at least seventeen stone, Eric was not a small man, and as I had tried to catch my breath, he had ripped away my bra, while his teeth bit into my now exposed and vulnerable breasts.

I had tried to scream, but with his hand still gripped around my throat it had come out only as a gargled groan. Thrashing violently on the bed, I could feel my energy draining away, my legs and arms felt weak, and my chest heaved with the strain of trying to push him from me. I had no fight left, and he knew that, he knew that he would win – he always won.

Feeling his hand down between my legs, I forced them

shut, momentarily trapping him, but he was stronger, and I had no strength left with which to fight him, I didn't stand a chance. As he pulled my knickers down over my knees and flipped me roughly over onto my stomach, I had prayed that it would be over quickly.

The pain that shot through my body as Eric had forced himself into me had taken my breath away, and as nausea had hit me, and my head began to spin I had vomited violently across his hand and forearm, the taste of bile burning the back of my throat making me gag.

'Bitch!' he had yelled, punching the back of my head with such force that my face bounced against the mattress, and I had felt darkness descending.

'Eric... please...' I had whimpered, 'Stop.'

But Eric did not stop.

Eric did not stop until he had finished with me. Only then did he drag me into the bathroom and dump me in the shower, spraying me with cold water until the vomit was no longer covering my face.

I had sat shivering and bruised as freezing water cascaded across my throbbing body, pleading with Eric to end this madness, but he did not hear me, he didn't want to hear me. He wanted only what he classed as *his right*.

Dragging me from the shower, he had thrown me to the

bathroom floor and slapped my face, 'wake up sleepyhead.' He laughed, 'I haven't finished with you yet!'

'Eric, please!' I screamed, desperately trying to move away from him, 'please stop!'

'I'll stop when I'm good and ready.' He had whispered menacingly into my ear. 'And I have so much more that I want to do to you, *Wife*!'

'Eric…' I groaned, as blackness once again began to cloud my vision, '…Eric, I…'

Clamping a hand across my mouth he had forced himself upon me once more, but I did not struggle. I laid perfectly still. I laid so still that he thought I had passed out.

'Bitch!' he hissed against my cheek as he climaxed, 'Fucking bitch!'

I hadn't even flinched as he kicked me in the ribs before slamming the bathroom door shut. But once I knew that he was gone, really gone, I curled up into a little ball and silently cried.

'Happy wedding day *Mrs Sawyer*…' I had wept to myself, '…here's to many more years to come.'

The following morning as I had showered, I inspected the bruises that covered my breasts, arms, legs and ribs, thankful that they were at least in places that could be

66

covered.

As I had quickly dressed in a floor-length, long-sleeved dress, popped four more painkillers and expertly applied makeup to my bruises, I had stood watching Eric sleeping for a little while, wondering how he could look so peaceful now, after the monster he had become.

I hadn't slept at all, fearful that he would wake and want another go at me, and so I had sat propped up against the bathroom door, not even daring to use the toilet. I knew that I had to stay quiet, I couldn't alert him to the fact that I was awake.

But he had not woken once, he had slept well, and when he finally did wake, he had been so sincere in his apologies that I knew that it must have been the emotions of the day, coupled with the amount of alcohol that he had consumed that had made him act so savagely.

I knew that he was sorry, I just knew it.

'Can you ever forgive me?' He whispered against my cheek, 'I am so sorry. I can't even begin to explain why I behaved in such an appalling manner – and on our wedding night too.'

'It's okay.' I had soothed, 'I know you had a lot to drink, so…'

'That doesn't excuse my behaviour, Jade. I hit you! Please

believe me when I say that it will never happen again.' He had smiled sadly at me, 'you do believe me, don't you?'

I had nodded, not daring to speak because I knew that even the smallest thing could set him off again, but then I also knew that I would forgive him anything, because everything that he was, I wanted.

'How can I make this up to you?' he had asked, desperate to make amends, 'just ask and it's yours.'

'I don't need anything.' I smiled. Though what I really needed more than anything was sleep and maybe a trip to a doctor. I felt certain that he had cracked one of my ribs when he kicked me.

'There must be something.' He had urged.

Desperate to end the conversation and move into less hostile territory, I grabbed my handbag and moved cautiously towards the door, 'well, breakfast would be nice.' I had ventured, even though the thought of eating anything made my stomach turn.

'Then breakfast it is Mrs Sawyer.' He grinned, 'I plan to spend the day making this up to you, so whatever you want to do we will do it.'

I knew that it would take more than one day of good deeds to make up for what he had done to me, but I also knew that I wouldn't pursue apologetic gifts and trinkets, because I didn't want this to drag on, I didn't want to run the risk of losing him.

I couldn't bear the thought of having my heart broken again, I couldn't bear the thought of hurting the way that Damon had hurt me, because I knew that I wasn't strong enough to come through it a second time.

I knew even then, as those thoughts had entered my brain that it was a pathetic excuse to stay with someone – but I also knew that I loved him, and a few bruises after one too many drinks would never change that. And yet, those pesky butterflies had returned, and this time they wouldn't be silenced.

Venice had been Eric's idea of the perfect honeymoon destination, and as we had unpacked our suitcases in our fully air-conditioned hotel room, I had had to agree - Venice was indeed perfect.

We were staying at the *Hotel Carlton* on the *Grand Canal*, and it was sumptuous. With its roof top cocktail bar and Venetian-style bedroom, it really was like stepping into a different world – it was simply divine.

It had been three weeks since our wedding, and thankfully the bruises that covered my body were now fading well enough for me to be able to cover them with makeup. Now nobody would ever know that they were there.

But I would know.

I would always know.

We couldn't leave right away for our honeymoon as Eric had work commitments that couldn't be rearranged – but he had been the perfect gentleman since our wedding day. He hadn't so much as raised his voice to me once – and as happy as that made me, it did also leave me wondering just how long this peace would last.

I hadn't seen the girls since the wedding – how could I with my face bruised and my pride dented? Heidi would have flipped if she had known what Eric had done to me, so I had communicated with them via text message and phone calls, and if I sent them photos, I ensured that I had run them through the editing app that I had on my phone first.

And my lame excuse for not seeing them when asked?

Well, I was busy with honeymoon prep of course! Pathetic, but it worked.

'So, what do you want to do first.' Eric had asked. Sliding his arms around my waist, 'a siesta?'

Chuckling I spun around to kiss him and suggest that we find the beach, there would be plenty of time for *siestas* later.

'Okay.' He grinned, 'if my wife wants the beach, then my wife shall have the beach.'

I had expected an argument. I had expected a flat-out refusal, that once again he would take what was *rightfully* his, but nope, Eric it would seem was still on his forgiveness mission.

I couldn't explain the change in Eric – but he had suddenly become *Mr Nice Guy*. Nothing was too much trouble for him, he no longer snapped at me or made snide comments – he was finally the Eric that I knew he could be, and I was finally happy to be married to him. If only he had been this way on our wedding day too.

'Did you pack sun-cream?' he had asked as he pulled his shorts on. 'I think the temperature out there is rising, it's already twenty-six degrees.'

'Sure did.' I had laughed, throwing the bottle his way, 'can't be having a crispy groom now, can we? Give me five mins to change, and I'll lather you up.' I had winked – which received me a cheeky wink in return. I was happy at that moment. So unbelievably happy.

Venice did not have a beach that was within walking distance of our hotel, meaning we would have to take a waterbus (*Vaporetto*), to reach *Alberoni beach* – so leaving

Eric to read the ingredients in the sun cream, (*he did things like that*), I headed to the bathroom and topped up the concealer on my bruises, aware that I would have to avoid swimming for a few more days, and slipped into my new hot pink bikini, knowing full well that it would make Eric's eyes pop the second he saw me – maybe the siesta might take precedence over the beach after all.

Giggling like a teenager, I sashayed across the bedroom floor and twirled in front of an open-mouthed Eric 'you like?' I had purred seductively.

Looking back, as I have done so many times over the years that followed, I should have known that his reaction would not be as I had hoped. That as he had dropped the bottle of sun cream onto the tiled floor and barrelled towards me, I should have run. But I didn't run, I had been rooted to the spot in fear, unsure why he had looked so angry – what had I done wrong now?

'What the hell is *that*?!' he had demanded, grabbing my arm and dragging me back into the bathroom, as I yelped in pain, 'what the hell do you think you look like? Are you trying to piss me off?'

Grabbing my chin, he forced me to look at myself in the mirror – and to this day I cannot understand what he saw that was so wrong.

72

I had a great figure, clear skin (*if you ignored the bruises*) long, clean hair, and the bikini wasn't *that* revealing! 'I don't understand.' I whimpered, 'I thought you would like it?'

'Oh, you thought I'd like other men ogling my wife at the beach, did you? You might as well as be naked!'

As he ripped the bikini from my body, leaving me trembling and naked before him I had begun to cry.

'Eric, please…'

'Do you intentionally do these things to push my buttons? Do you enjoy getting a rise out of me?' Ignoring my tears, he had thrown a robe at me and told me to cover myself up, 'I suppose *I'll* have to find you something more suitable to wear, won't I!'

'But what is wrong with the bikini?' I had dared to ask, 'everybody else will be wearing one.'

'Everybody else isn't my wife!' he had thundered. 'And tie back your hair, it looks a damned mess – you know I prefer short hair on women!'

He had stormed from the room then, and I had crumpled to the floor, crying tears that I thought were finally gone forever.

He had never once expressed an opinion regarding hair length, not once. So why now? Did he no longer find me attractive? My hair had always been my best feature, and despite having it trimmed regularly it was now almost to my waist. I loved my hair.

I would not cut it. Not even for him.

When he returned some two hours later, he had smelt of whisky and had thrown a blue plastic bag at me.

'Put that on and be quick about it – otherwise, we will never make it to the bloody beach!'

I didn't dare tell him that I no longer wanted to go and instead pulled on the full bathing suit that he had purchased for me.

Navy blue and cut in such a way that a nun would feel completely covered, I had held back the tears that were once again threatening to fall – I had never felt so unattractive in my whole life. How could I venture out wearing this? How could he think this was suitable for a honeymoon?

'See?' he had smiled, taking me in his arms, 'isn't that so much better?'

I nodded, because really, what else could I have done?

'I got you this as well.'

This was a pale blue sarong, which in all honestly wasn't the worst part of the outfit that he had chosen, and it had allowed me to cover up most of the disgusting bathing suit.

Thanking him, I pulled my hair into a messy bun, grabbed my beach bag, slipped my feet into my flip-flops and headed for the door, knowing that the day could not possibly improve.

'You look beautiful Jade.' He had stated matter of factly, 'let's hit the beach, eh?'

I didn't look beautiful, I looked frumpy – but maybe in some small way, it had been Eric's way of protecting me? Eric's way of ensuring that other men didn't get the wrong idea about me?

The butterflies did not agree.

The rest of our honeymoon passed in relative harmony as we spent lazy afternoons on the beach, long hot days visiting the tourist attractions - we rode the *Grand Canal* in a gondola, visited *St. Mark's Basilica*, *Piazza San Marco* and the *Bridge of Sighs* – it was all stunning – and yet I felt so alone.

I didn't feel like a happy bride on her honeymoon, so in love, - I felt trapped – like my reactions to these beautiful places were just an act, and I hated that. I hated Eric for making me feel that way.

Why couldn't he just be normal?

Why couldn't he just behave rationally?

Eric had ruined our wedding night and he had ruined our honeymoon, and yet a part of me blamed myself. I should have known that the pink bikini would not sit right with him. Did I do it intentionally? Did I wear it on purpose? Is he right in saying that I purposely push his buttons?

Maybe.

Maybe not.

With Eric, it was difficult to know.

Eventually, our fortnight in Venice was over, and before I knew it, we were back home, catching up with the lives that had briefly stood still, awaiting our return.

I had mixed emotions about being home. At least in Venice, I knew it was all an act – but here – now – it was real. This was my new life, and I had brought it all on myself.

As I had feared, Eric did not return to the loving man that he had briefly become and instead was a permanent monster. I was terrified of him. I was genuinely terrified of him.

I found myself walking on eggshells whenever he was around, constantly worried that I would say or do the wrong thing. That I would accidentally trigger his anger and suffer yet another beating.

Eric didn't always hit me though. He didn't need to. His

cruel words were often enough to beat me down. But on the days that his anger truly reached boiling point, his fists would not know when to stop.

Of course, he was always apologetic afterwards – showering me with gifts and flowers, and I of course accepted it – I of course accepted the excuses.

He was stressed at work.

He was exhausted.

He was under a lot of pressure.

And I of course could not possibly understand.

I no longer saw my friends, which in a way was easier for me, because at least that way I wouldn't have to try and explain the bruises. Nobody would believe that I had walked into a cupboard door for the fifth time, even I wasn't that clumsy.

I know that I should have asked for help, I know that I should have left him – but I did love him, I did.

I was allowed to see my parents every second Sunday, and on those days, I would ensure that my makeup was heavily applied, one to cover any lingering bruises, and two to hide the dark circles that lived permanently beneath my eyes.

Eric always came with me when I visited them, and my parents still believed that he was wonderful. So many times I had tried to tell them – so many times I had opened my mouth fully intent on letting them know just how wonderful he was not, but then he would be there – his fingers digging into my shoulder, glaring at me – because he knew – he knew that I wanted out.

But still, I loved him.

I loved him although he criticised every little thing that I did…

His meal wasn't hot enough.

His coffee not strong enough.

The bathroom not clean enough.

I haven't closed the blinds correctly.

I accidentally hung a black shirt in with the blue.

I wore something that he deemed inappropriate.

I left crumbs on the kitchen counter.

The list was endless of stupid, petty things that he could throw at me, but the night that he came home drunk after hours of partying with his friends, to find me reading in bed, was the night that my love for him eventually began to fade. And even though there had been nights before that were much worse, something triggered inside of me that night, and I knew that I could take no more.

When Eric went out with his friends, I had to wait up for him, because despite him staying out until all hours having fun, I had to make sure that I was presentable, no matter the time, and that I was ready for him, waiting willingly for him to take again what he classed as rightfully his.

I had to ensure that I was wearing the red lingerie set that he had bought me and that I was standing by the front door, eager for his return.

It didn't matter if I had had a long day or if I was tired. *No!*

I was there to service him, and god help me if I was not ready.

Well, that night I was not ready. That night I was fed up with waiting around for a husband that was no doubt flirting with every woman that he could get his hands on – while his pathetic wife waited patiently at home for him.

I had decided at midnight to call it a night. He clearly had no intention of coming home, and even if he did, by that point he would be too drunk to notice me anyway.

How wrong I was.

At 1.17 A.M. I heard our front door slam shut, and a drunken Eric stumbling around the kitchen. I ignored him and carried on reading my book, he would no doubt pass out on the sofa anyway, so why should I bother getting up. I didn't hear Eric approach the bedroom door, but as he suddenly appeared looming largely in the doorway and swaying ever so slightly, I knew in an instant that I was in trouble.

'Reading?' he had snarled, 'what have I told you about reading!'

Eric didn't like it when I filled my head with nonsensical fiction stories – he said that they gave women like me the wrong idea about life and that I should instead read books based on true events. But I enjoyed fiction, I enjoyed the only thing in my life that gave me some form of escapism. Grabbing the book from my hand, Eric ripped it right down the middle, and then threw it into the corner of the bedroom, before launching himself onto the bed beside me. Part of me at that moment could only think of how grateful I was that the book wasn't completely destroyed and that I would just need to tape it back together to make it whole again.

If only I were so easily mended.

'Where were you *wife*?!' he had demanded to know, as his beer breath wafted across towards me, 'Not in your usual spot I see.'

'I was just tired tonight Eric; I just fancied an early night.'

'But you were reading? That's hardly an early night is it.' He smiled, touching my cheek ever so gently. 'If you were tired you should have gone to sleep.'

'Well, I tried, but I found that I couldn't sleep right away, so I thought I'd...'

'Read?' he mocked. 'You thought you'd neglect your husband and read!'

'No, I...'

'Get up!' he suddenly yelled at me, as he pulled the covers from the bed. 'What the hell are you wearing?' he demanded to know, taking in my nightwear with disgust. I hadn't dressed in the lingerie at all as Eric preferred, instead, I had on my Bambi pyjamas that Heidi had bought me a few years back for my birthday, 'what the hell are those!'

'Pyjamas.' I squeaked, nervously.

'Pyjamas! When have I ever said that you can sleep in pyjamas? It's either the lingerie that I buy you or nothing Jade, it sure as shit isn't pyjamas that a bloody child would wear!'

'Eric...'

'Strip! I want you in the red knickers and bra, now!'

'Eric, come on, it's the middle of the night.' I pleaded, 'let's just sleep, okay.'

'STRIP!' he screamed, yanking at my pyjama bottoms with unsteady hands. 'You know the rules!'

All too aware now that I would not escape this night unscathed, I removed my pyjamas and moved across to the wardrobe to locate the hideous red lingerie.

'Stop!' he commanded, as I turned slowly to look at him. 'I think I want you to dance for me instead.'

'Oh, Eric.' I had laughed anxiously, 'you know I'm no good at that sort of thing. I'll just put the underwear on instead, then we can…'

'I said DANCE!'

Feeling myself burn with utter humiliation I began to sway from side to side, trying my hardest not to cry – why was he doing this to me!

'You're right.' He mocked, 'you can't dance! It's like watching a half-dead fish flopping about on the sand! Christ, you know how to turn a man off!'

'Shall we just sleep then?' I had dared to ask.

The slap came out of nowhere. I hadn't even seen him move from the bed.

'Did I say anything about sleeping?'

'But you just said…'

'If you start blubbering on me then this is going to get a whole lot worse for you! Now put the red stuff on and do your job!'

With trembling hands, I reached inside the wardrobe and

pulled out the flimsy red material that Eric seemed to enjoy so much, and clumsily began to fasten the bra.

'Are you trying to piss me off? Just put it on already!'

'I'm trying.'

'Do you need me to dress you, like a little baby?'

Sobbing, I dropped the bra to the floor and ran for the bathroom, I couldn't do it, I just couldn't.

'JADE!' he screamed, 'Don't make me come in there and get you!'

Shaking violently, I had put my full weight against the bathroom door, knowing all the while that it and the flimsy lock would not keep him out.

'Just leave me alone.' I had howled, 'Please!'

'I want what is mine, *wife*!'

'You can't just demand this of me.' I yelled, 'I'm not your plaything, you psycho!'

'Come out of there Jade. You're only making things worse for yourself.'

'Screw you! I'm not coming anywhere near you ever again! You can consider this marriage well and truly dissolved!'

'What did you just say?'

I had remained silent then, knowing that I had gone too far – knowing that he would never let me go.

'Did you just threaten to leave me? You don't ever get to leave – you hear me!'

I had not responded, even as he began punching the door, I had remained still. I knew that he was capable of hurting me, he had done so already on many occasions – but at that moment I truly believed that he would also be capable of killing me.

How had it all come to this?

How had one chance meeting in a bar come to this? I should have listened to my head right at the start and not been overruled by my stupid love desperate heart.

'Jade! Open this door right now!'

As Eric had begun to kick at the door I had screamed until my lungs burnt, petrified and all too aware that once he came barrelling through that door I was in big trouble.

'Jade!', he continued to scream as the door finally gave way and splintered open with a deafening crack. Scrambling frantically away from him, I struggled against not only my fear but the slippiness of the bathroom tiles, I was like a sitting duck as the high gloss flooring refused to give my feet any traction.

'You don't get to hide from me Jade, ever!' he had roared as he lunged for me, 'You want to run away from me? Well, know this – I would find you, *wife*! I would find you no matter how far you ran!'

'Eric!' I had sobbed, as I sat there paralysed by fear, 'Eric, I'm sorry! I am so so sorry!'

He had lunged for me then, and I could feel my hair being ripped painfully from my scalp as he dragged me across the cold bathroom tiles and back into the bedroom. 'You want to play games Jade?' he had screamed at me, while raining punches against my head and body, 'let's see how you like these games shall we!'

I swear that sometimes Eric was testing himself, to see just how far he was prepared to go in his destruction of me, and I knew that one day he would go too far. That one day I would be dead by his hand. And I knew, I just knew that even if he did kill me, he would get away with it. People like him always get away with it.

I had tried to curl myself up into a little ball, to close myself off from his abuse, as I had done so many times in the past – but this time was different. This time I was unable to shut my mind off, such was the pain that he was inflicting upon me.

I had tried to protect myself by shielding my head and my body, but he would rip my arms away from my face and slap me until I was near to unconsciousness.

He knew how to prolong his torture of me.

He knew how to hurt me but not enough that I would black out and ruin his fun.

It had seemed as though the punching, kicking and slapping had taken hours, but in fact, it had been mere minutes.

When he had finally stopped, to catch his breath, I had stupidly believed that it was all over – that he had *taught me my lesson* – But I was wrong.

He had raped me then.

But it hadn't been quick, it hadn't been easy to block out, and it hadn't been just the once.

After each attack he would drag me to the shower and watch as I cleaned myself, relishing in my total humiliation. And just when I thought that he was done with me, he would beat me again and drag me back to the bedroom.

Screaming inside, I knew that I had to get away from this monster – that no matter the consequences of my actions I had to try and escape.

I was already living on borrowed time.

'**I**'m just going to pop into town and grab a few last bits for Christmas.' I smiled nervously, as Eric looked me up and down. 'I won't be long.'

It had been three weeks since he had attacked me in the bathroom, and while my wounds were healing well, Eric's abuse of me had not relented.

He had found new excuses to beat me, new reasons to justify his insane behaviour.

His coffee was too hot.

I hadn't cooked his steak exactly how he likes it.

I hadn't loaded the dishwasher correctly.

I hadn't emptied the dishwasher.

I hadn't made the bed to military precision.

I hadn't ironed his shirt correctly.

I didn't immediately rise when the alarm went off.

His eggs were runny, his toast too dark, his pillows not plumped, his toothbrush not charged...

It was endless and it was stupid.

'You have one hour!' he smirked, enjoying the time restrictions that he imposed upon my life. 'One hour exactly!'

I had nodded, not trusting myself to speak. Not because I had some smart-mouthed response ready and waiting, no. I dared not open my mouth for fear of saying the wrong thing, thus giving him the perfect excuse to put an end to my outing.

'You don't speak to anybody – you hear me? You go to

the shop, get what you need and come straight back home!'

Nodding again, I grabbed my bag, reluctantly kissed my husband and headed out. Even though I only had one hour, I planned to savour every moment.

I had been tempted to pop by and see Heidi – but despite my makeup covering the last of the bruises on my face, they were still obvious – it was still evident that I had been beaten.

So, I instead wrapped my scarf closer around my face and made my way towards the town centre to try and find Eric a Christmas gift.

He didn't deserve one.

He would also hate whatever I bought for him, so I didn't plan to put too much effort into it.

Whitby was bitterly cold in Winter, as the wind blew in across the harbour, but it was also so magical. Christmas lights adorned the shop windows, twinkling away merrily, as people wandered around, laughing and feeling festive. I wanted more than one hour – I wanted the whole day! I wanted to be just like those people. Those happy, lost in the moment, feeling festive people.

But I wasn't like them – and I never would be again.

Making my way immediately to *The Whitby Bookshop*,

I debated mentally whether or not Eric would appreciate a book for Christmas? Nothing fictional of course, but an autobiography maybe? I also planned to pick up something for myself, which I would hide in the plant pot by the front door until Eric went to the pub – what he didn't know wouldn't inevitably hurt me.

I hadn't immediately seen Heidi as I had passed the *White Horse and Griffin* pub – a place that I tended to avoid, as Eric and his mates drank in there regularly – and I knew that he would no doubt have his friends spying on me.

As our eyes met across the crowds gathering outside of the pub, I made a run for it. Cowardly and stupid I know, but I couldn't face seeing her – I couldn't bear for her to see me like this.

'Jade!' she had yelled, picking up the pace behind me. 'Jade, wait!'

I had run then, so fast, across the swing bridge, dodging out of the way of the Christmas shoppers, trying desperately not to knock them over. I had no idea where I was running to, I just knew that I had to get away from Heidi, I had to escape her prying eyes.

'Jade!'

I hadn't seen the car as I raced across New Quay Road,

but I had felt it as it ploughed into me, sending me soaring weightlessly through the sky, only to land with a sickening crunch on the roadside.

Jade had caught up with me then – and as my body had slowly powered down, I had heard only the distant echo of her screams and the shocked exclamations of strangers, desperate to turn their faces away from the horror before them, but powerless to stop their eyes wandering back.

'Call an ambulance!'

'She just came out of nowhere!'

'I didn't even see her!'

'She was running from something! She damn near knocked me and the missus over on the bridge!'

'Is she dead?'

'Okay, okay, let's give her some space, c'mon, move back!'

'Jade? Jade, don't you dare die on me!'

I knew then that I should have just stopped.

I should have let her rest her eyes upon my fading bruises. No matter the consequences.

I should have just admitted that she was right all along.

PART TWO

MY PRESENT, MY FUTURE...

'You have a blunt force spinal cord injury, Mrs Sawyer.'

Those were the first words that the surgeon spoke to me five months ago, after waking me from the induced coma that I was in for four months.

Oh, how I wish that he hadn't bothered to wake me. I was happy in my forced slumber, I was dreaming, beautiful dreams, peaceful dreams.

But then I woke, and there he was.

Eric!

Looming over my bed, his face a mask of insincere concern - his crocodile tears a joke!

'Thank God, Jade, you are awake! I have been so worried about you!'

I knew though that he wouldn't have wasted any of his precious time fretting over whether I would make it or not – and I doubted very much that he spent his nights alone wishing that I was sleeping beside him. *No, not Eric.*

He no doubt had a different woman every night comforting him in *his* hour of need. But I'll just bet his performance of *the worried husband* in front of my parents would have won him an Oscar!

I imagine the only thing that Eric was truly put out about, was that he had temporarily lost his punchbag!

It was explained to me that I was placed into an

induced coma after being hit by the car to minimize brain swelling and inflammation, such were the extent of my injuries, and it appears that I had not wanted to wake back up.

Well, can you blame me, really?

I had broken my right arm, left wrist, left ankle, and fractured five ribs in the accident, as well as suffering substantial head trauma, but I count myself lucky, as my body had healed as I had slept – I made it, somehow, I made it.

They apparently tried quite a few times to bring me round, but I flat-out refused. I'm surprised Eric didn't just order them to pull the plug!

I can remember the accident in crystal clear clarity, and I know that I was stupid just running out into the road like that – but in all honesty, I think the bang to my head did me some good – it has made me see things clearly for the first time in a long time.

It has made me realise that I do want to live. But not like this – not with him!

So here I am – it's May, two thousand and twenty-two, I missed Christmas and Easter, and I'm confined to a wheelchair, though I plan for this to be a very temporary inconvenience in my life.

I still plan to leave Eric – that decision is still very much firm in my mind, and despite this now being a new setback, I will get out of here. I will.

For that very reason, I haven't told anybody that I have regained some feeling in my legs.

Eric did initially, for the first few weeks, take me to physio, but once he saw that I was not recovering as quickly as he wanted me to, he abruptly ended the sessions, declaring somewhat loudly and proudly that he would pay for a private physiotherapist to come to the house.

That person has never appeared!

I have however taken what I learnt ever so briefly from my physio sessions and worked out my own exercise plan. I can now, somewhat shakily, stand for short periods.

It's gruelling and it's painful – but I need to be strong.

Eric does not know.

He will never know.

I wait until he leaves the house before I begin my exercises, and once he returns, I sit as still as I possibly can in my wheelchair so as not to arouse suspicion.

Eric may still be abusing me, but for once I hold some of the cards, and this time I will come out on top.

Currently, I am unable to leave the house as my

wheelchair and the stairs outside are not a particularly good mix - and Eric? Well, he doesn't exactly go out of his way to ensure that I get fresh air and a change of scenery as the doctors ordered – though he pretends that he does.

My parents visit regularly, as do the girls, as Eric has not yet discovered a way in which to prevent this from happening, so he goes along with it – for now at least. For a brief moment, I felt that I had won a small battle, that there was something - just a tiny something that he could not control – but my victory was short-lived, and as I run my hands across my head, I sob. Eric had taken scissors to my long, beautiful hair one night as I slept, and he has forbidden me to grow it long again. Even though I know it's only hair, it's like he removed another part of me.

Heidi had been shocked to see my hair, and I had quickly explained that it was much easier this way, much more manageable – she had scolded Eric then, saying that she would have come by to wash my hair, look after my personal needs (*she had, of course, noticed my somewhat dishevelled appearance*) – he had shrugged, said it was just hair, and who saw me anyway? But I had seen something flash across his face, and I knew instantly that he was fully aware at that moment that he had made a big mistake. Eric knew that he could not afford for anybody to realise just how badly he was treating me, and from that moment on when visitors were due, he would ensure that I was dressed, my makeup was applied and that I looked cared for.

It was all a disguise of course. His devoted behaviour, my ironed clothes, perfumed skin, make-up – because when they left again, and it was just me and him, he would roughly scrub the makeup from my face, and I would be dumped back into the spare bedroom where I would spend the remainder of the day and night alone.

Eric of course still had *his needs*, and though I know that these are met outside of our marriage, he still drags me from the spare bedroom, into the main bedroom for sex as and when he desires. I am not permitted to stay in the main bedroom once the deed is done, however. I am dumped unceremoniously into my wheelchair and plunged once more into solitude.

Those moments I am thankful for.

He bathes me only when he can be bothered to, which is not often enough – and so I must wait again once more until he leaves the house before I can wash properly.

I dare not use the bath or the shower, I cannot risk being caught, or in my rush to complete the task, leave evidence of my ability to function without him. So, I make do with full body washes using nothing but a bar of soap, a flannel and hot water in the sink.

Eric hates the fact that he now has a disabled wife, something which he tells me almost daily – and it angers me because he put me here. I am in this wheelchair because of him!

Maybe he didn't force me in front of that car – but his actions and my fear of him did!

Heidi in her eagerness to bring back the *old me*, had on one surprise visit when Eric was not around, handed me a small parcel, a parcel that contained false nails, mascara, face cream and a tube of red lipstick. I had looked upon that tiny tube of red lipstick in delight. Knowing wickedly that Eric hated red lips, knowing that if he caught me with it that I would be in all kinds of trouble. So, I applied it when he wasn't around when it was just me, the wheelchair, my balcony view and the never-ending relentless silence.

I would look at myself in my small hand-held mirror and imagine that I *was* the old me, that I *was* the woman that laughed freely, danced until her feet ached, and took pleasure in quiet nights in and rowdy nights out. But then I would see past the lipstick and the now short hair and realise that I no longer recognised myself. I don't know who that person is that stares back at me with big sad eyes. I just know that she is incredibly unhappy.

One particular day I felt restless, I felt disobedient, I felt reckless, and I had taken that shocking red lipstick and slowly brushed it against my chapped lips, imagining just for a moment that I was getting ready for a big night out with the girls – it had been a few moments of pure fantasy – until he came home unexpectedly!

When he saw the lipstick on my lips, he froze, then launched himself across the room towards me – grabbing me by my head he dragged me out of my wheelchair and into the bathroom, forcing my head under the taps. I couldn't breathe as he roughly scrubbed the lipstick from my mouth, screaming all the while that I was cheap and dirty, a whore! I had dared not move, through fear, understandably, but also, because I could not let him see that I had any movement whatsoever in my legs.

Things with Eric had escalated to a dangerous level since that last night in the bathroom, and I knew that one day he would kill me.

Afterwards, as I had sat dripping wet and trembling on the floor, my teeth chattering against the cold, he had slammed the door and not returned for twelve hours. I had not dared to stand and make my way back into my wheelchair, I had not dared to make any attempt to leave the bathroom – what if it was all a trick and he was really standing outside the door? What if he was spying on me? Those were the kind of sick jokes that he liked to play – he could not be trusted.

I have risked the lipstick since and have not been caught, which leads me to believe that he thinks I am too scared now, and I am, believe me, but if I'm ever to escape this hell then I need to start taking chances, no matter the consequence.

I have risked standing on my balcony looking out to sea wearing nothing but a white chiffon night dress, imagining that I am free, that I can come and go as I please. That I am just like the holiday makers having fun on the beach, strolling hand in hand with their loved ones, eating ice cream and hunting for seashells - but when I take off the dress and re-hide it, I become all too aware once again that I am not.

One day I will leave. Just me and my suitcase – and the holidaymakers and sandcastle builders will be totally oblivious to my plight – just as they are now.

Eric is completely oblivious to the fact that I have a suitcase. Not just any old suitcase. No. This suitcase holds what remains of Jade Locke, and it will be the only thing that I take with me when I finally escape.

Inside my secret suitcase, which is hidden deep at the back of the spare bedroom wardrobe, beneath old blankets and bedding, I have my old clothes, from my old life, that I managed to hide away from Eric - my MP3 player, two pairs of shoes, a pair of trainers and a pair of boots, photographs of my friends on various nights out, my makeup – which is sadly out of date now, some bits of jewellery, a winter coat, my handbag and purse and my old mobile phone.

I don't use my mobile phone, and I would never risk him finding it – but just knowing that I have it, that when I'm free, I have some way of contacting people is enough to give me some much-needed inner strength.

I wish that I could just walk out of the front door right now, suitcase in hand and be away from him forever. Or that I could phone Heidi or my parents and have them come get me – but that wouldn't be well planned enough, and I can't put my friends and family in the path of a madman.

My plan needs to be so well executed and fine-tuned that he can never ever find me. I can't tell anybody what I am doing or where I am going, because Eric would find out. They would try not to tell him of course, but he would get it out of them eventually.

What Eric wants; Eric gets.

I am mentally prepared to go.

I have a plan that I believe will set me free.

And I have never been so scared in my life.

It's mid-morning, and Eric has just discovered that my period has once again arrived on time, never a day early, never a day late – he monitors them each month, and this month his anger and frustration at its arrival are instant.

'I just don't understand Jade, how can you be on your period again! This is getting beyond a joke – there's clearly something wrong with you!'

'There's nothing wrong with me. Some couples just take a while to conceive that's all.' I argue back, determined not to have this fall in my lap again, 'My body has suffered serious trauma, Eric, it's still healing. I'm sure it will happen one day.'

'One day isn't good enough!' he snaps, angrily, 'Clearly *you* have problems!'

I know better than to say that maybe the fault is his, after all, the perfect God-like man that is Eric Sawyer could never be infertile.

'Well arguing about it won't help the situation, will it?' I dare to respond, knowing full well that Eric hates it when I answer back, 'all we can do is keep trying.' I smile, even though the thought of Eric touching me makes my skin crawl.

'No! That's not good enough, we need to see a specialist! Your accident might have damaged something inside of you, we need to know!'

Taken aback by his concern, I am momentarily lost for words.

'Oh, don't be getting any romantic notions in your stupid head, I need to know if you can give me kids or not, if you're broken then that's *your* problem!'

'Surely it would be your problem also, would it not?' I dare to question, as I hand him a perfect cup of coffee, not too hot, not too milky. I am battered from all angles and yet still I play the perfect wife – cooking, cleaning, and making the perfect bloody coffee!

'*My* problem?' he snarls, slamming the coffee cup down onto the dining table, 'if you can't get knocked up how is that my problem?'

'But you want children?' I ask confused, 'so if I am unable to conceive then it would be a joint problem – wouldn't it?' Raising my chin defiantly, all too aware that his temper is almost at the tipping point, I smile as sweetly as

I can muster at the man that I despise. 'Wouldn't it?'

'Who said I needed *you* to carry *my* child? If you're damaged goods, then I'll just find a woman that isn't.'

'Wow! That's a new low even for you! So just any old womb will do, will it?' I snap, even though I am not totally sure why – if he has a baby with somebody else then that frees me from his wandering hands.

'She won't be old; I can assure you.' He grins.

'You would just have a baby with another woman despite our still being married?'

'*Still* being married?' he questions, with a raised eyebrow, 'we will *always* be married, Jade.'

Scoffing, I wheel a little further away from him, 'Oh yeah, sure, we play happy families while you knock some other woman up – just what I always wanted.'

Laughing he picks up his cup, sneering at the ring that he's left on the table, just long enough for me to notice and immediately clean it away, 'You will do as I say Jade Sawyer – you are mine now, and you will accept and obey my decisions.'

'So, you do whatever you want, and I just sit here in my chair, slowly dying – is that it? Is that the marriage you wanted Eric!'

'No.' he begins, slowly, 'I wanted a wife that would do as

she was told, that would look after me, look after our home, our kids – but what did I get Jade?' He yells suddenly, grabbing my wheelchair and pulling me closer, 'I get a cripple that can't even get pregnant! I should just put you out of your misery right now.'

'Do it then!' I scream as I try to manoeuvre my chair even closer to him, 'do it now! Just kill me! I mean can you even trust me to look after your precious child if I'm so useless?!' I instantly regret the words as he throws lukewarm coffee into my face and drags my head backwards by my hair.

'If by some small miracle, your wrecked body does get pregnant, know this – if you *ever* do anything to harm my child it will be the last thing you ever do! Understood?! Now clean yourself up, you're a mess!'

Nodding meekly, and too afraid now to push him any further, I manoeuvre my wheelchair into the bathroom to wash my face, my eyes falling instantly upon the Tampax box in the corner.

God if he ever knew.

'I'll be back late, don't bother waiting up!' he calls out as the door slams heavily behind him.

Gone now are the nights when I was forced to wait patiently for his return in cheap red lingerie, no matter the hour. And while it hasn't stopped him from seeking me out, desperate to impregnate me – it is at least not as often as it used to be.

Waiting until the front door slams shut and his whistling fades into the distance, I carefully open the box of tampons and sigh in relief. They are still there – he hasn't found them, and all of this talk of specialists isn't a trick, as I had momentarily believed.

But I need a safer place to keep them, it's getting too dangerous now. If Eric ever finds out that I'm secretly taking the pill he will go ballistic!

It was easy to get the pill without him knowing. The doctor had given me a twelve-month supply at my last visit, which thankfully meant that I didn't have to create fictitious reasons for attending the clinic for more – not that Eric would have cared enough to accompany me anyway.

The problem that I now face is seeing an actual specialist for a problem that just doesn't exist. They will know won't they, from blood tests or something that I'm taking contraception? What if they mention it in front of him? There will be no way on this earth that he will let me go in alone for the results – he will be much too keen to be proven right, that I am indeed the one with the problem!

God help me if ever finds out!

I can't even begin to imagine his anger – despite being on the receiving end of it so many times – if he knew – it would be the end of me.

I need to be gone before this can ever be revealed.

Am I strong enough?

Well, I'll just have to be!

Splashing cold water across my face, I smile weakly at my reflection. I can do this – I can get out of this marriage from hell, and my legs – well, my shaky legs will carry me, I know they will. I just have to keep up with the exercises, build muscle, and gain strength – I will crawl if I have to. Drying my face, I jump as the doorbell rings – I'm not expecting anybody – Eric hasn't approved any visitations. Flopping heavily into my wheelchair I steer myself to the front door and am surprised to see Heidi standing there.

'Look.' she begins, hands in the air, as dramatic as always, 'I know you think that cutting your hair off is easier, right? But you loved that hair, and I feel terrible that I left you feeling like you couldn't manage it. So…' jazz hands now, '…I've bought you these.'

These are hair extensions. Jesus christ – how am I

supposed to tell her, without telling her, that if I attach these things to my head Eric will just rip them out – literally.

'Oh.' I smile, 'erm… thanks?'

'I know, I know.' She laughs, pushing my chair back into the lounge and sitting down in front of me, 'they're not the same as your real hair, but it's not a bad substitute until it grows back.'

'I…'

'Don't worry about washing and styling, I will come every day and help you with that, okay?'

'I can't ask you to do that – it's too much – you're busy and I'm… well, not obviously – but I'm used to the short hair now, I actually like it.'

'Jade… c'mon, what kind of a best friend would I be if I didn't recognise that you miss your hair.'

'Honestly, Heidi, I'm fine – really.'

'Can't you just let me help you?' she pleads, hands planted together as if in prayer.

'Help me with what?' I ask, 'My hair isn't short because of you, it's short because I want it short – honestly, one day I will grow it back – and then you can wash and style it as much as you like.'

Knowing how stubborn I can be, she sighs and places the

extensions in my lap – 'Okay, well I'm not giving up on this – you'll come around.' She winks, 'I just know that you will. I suppose if we aren't having a hair day we could go out. How about a spin around the pier and a cold ice cream on a bloody cold day?

Grimacing I find that I cannot look my oldest friend in the face, how many times can I say no before she stops asking? How long before she gives up on me?

'You know…' I begin, slowly, 'I haven't been feeling so well lately, I think I should stay home and rest.'

'Have you ever thought that the reason you feel like this is that you are practically locked away like a prisoner! Fresh air might be just what you need.'

'I'm not a prisoner Heidi.' I lie, 'I just don't feel ready to face the world yet – maybe next time?'

Can you just imagine the scene – Eric comes home early – which he has a very nasty habit of doing, only to find me gone – so he hunts me down – which he will do, only to find me munching on ice cream with my best friend – who he detests. Oh sure, he would be polite – to a point – with Heidi, but once home? Well – I dare not imagine.

'Is everything okay Jade? With… you know… Him?'

NO! I want to scream!

NO! It's torture, he tortures me!

NO! Save me, please. Oh god, save me!

'Everything is fine.' I smile sweetly. 'Absolutely fine.'

'You can talk to me you know – I can't promise that I won't go to town on your husband, but…'

'Honestly, Heidi, I'm really fine.'

'Okay.' She sighs, reluctantly, 'So, no hair, no outside, no talk, shall we just watch some telly?'

'You don't have to do this you know.' I smile, sadly, 'I'm sure you have a million other interesting things to be getting on with.'

'Hey!' she frowns, 'this *is* interesting for me – so don't you be getting any ideas about getting rid of me, okay? – best friends don't ditch each other – even if one of them is a total div when it comes to crossing the road.'

I laugh, because what else can I do?

Alone once more, I imagine the day that Heidi and the girls are back in my life. I imagine the day that I have a life again – I know that I should not dream such things, not until I have escaped, not until I'm in a position where I am in control of my own destiny – but I need these dreams – I need this hope! I know that it will be a long time before I can safely contact the girls once I am free – I know that I need to ensure that Eric has well and truly given up looking for me before I can even consider dragging them into my new life, whatever that new life looks like! Right now though, I need to imagine it, I need to be able to feel it, and I need to know that one day it will be possible.

I want to laugh again, to drink alcohol, sing oh so badly on karaoke night at *The Dirty Rabbit*, dress like me, not this frumpy stuff that Eric has me wearing – I want a job, a social media account, red lipstick, high heels, legs that work, freedom - I want a goddam life!

I wanted to ask after Nicky and Jess, I wanted to ask what they'd all been up to. Had they had any crazy nights out, drunken karaoke sessions, what colour Jessica's hair was this week – but I held back. Maybe that is selfish of me, not to ask after my friends, but it hurts. It hurts to know that life outside of these four walls goes on as normal for everybody else – whereas my life has changed beyond recognition.

How can meeting one person destroy everything?

How does that one person do that?

Well, they chip away at you slowly. The sly comments, the derogatory remarks, so by the time the first slap comes you almost feel as though you deserve it.

I should have walked out of that restaurant the second Eric

110

judged my food choice – better still, I should never have responded to his incessant text messages!

Hindsight as they say is a wonderful thing, but so is not being a stupid lovestruck fool!

I have a plan.

When my grandma passed away, she left me a lot of money – a big chunk of which I used to buy this house – the house of my dreams, now, just a house of nightmares. The remainder of the money I left tucked away in my savings account – an account that Eric thankfully has no idea about.

I haven't been idle in my efforts to escape Eric; I have been planning daily. I breathe this plan, I dream this plan, I *am* this plan.

Using the mobile phone that I found tucked away in my suitcase, I scoured the internet for car sales that would allow me to purchase a vehicle online and have it delivered to a location of my choice. I did find such a place and have managed to source a vehicle that is not flashy, not too new and shiny, and will not stand out like a sore thumb at my delivery point.

I asked them to leave my car, a blue Ford Fiesta, parked in the car park at the top of the one hundred and ninety-nine steps – opposite Whitby Abbey and to leave the keys taped under the driver's side wheel arch. They asked no questions, and I offered no explanations.

Sure, I could take a bus, maybe even a few trains – but those options leave me at the mercy of other people, traffic, and potential disruptions – I need to leave under my own steam – I need to know that when I get in that car I am on my way to my new life. I cannot allow anything to blindside me.

'**I**'ve managed to get *you* an appointment with a specialist at the end of November – dumb bitch receptionist wouldn't give me anything sooner!' Eric growls as he throws his jacket and tie over the back of the settee.

Nodding, I pick up his discarded clothing and muse that it's probably his piss poor attitude that has made that the case, and muse again that I am for once thankful that he has the temperament of an angry wasp, as it never seems to get him anywhere. 'November is okay.' I smile, 'It's not too far away.'

I need to leave before November!

'No point in wasting weeks not trying though is there.' He grins while eyeballing my breasts. 'If you manage to do what you're *supposed* to do and get pregnant then it might save us the hassle.'

Cringing inwardly, I wheel my chair towards the master bedroom, praying that he is quick.

'Where the hell do you think you're going?' he demands, pulling my wheelchair backwards.

'You just said...'

'Christ! You definitely got the looks but not the brains didn't you! Did I say that I wanted to have sex right this second? Did I say that?'

'No. I just thought...'

'Don't think Jade – you're not very good at it.' He sneers, 'What I want is my evening meal, and I don't smell anything cooking.'

Shit! I have been so consumed with daydreaming and Heidi's visit that I completely forgot to put the tea on. 'I thought we might go out?' I suggest meekly, 'we haven't done that for so long, and I...'

The slap hits my cheek so forcibly that my teeth smack against each other with a sickening crunch, 'what did I just say about thinking?'

'I'm sorry... I...'

'Get in that kitchen now and get my food on the table! Some of us around here work for a living you know! Christ, what does a man have to do to come home to a loving wife and a hot meal on the table?'

'I can't exactly work right now, Eric. I wish that I could.'

'I don't need this Jade. I don't need to be coming in from a hard day's work only to have you provoke and push me. I don't understand why you have to push my buttons, why you have to start arguments with me. Is it too much to just come home and you ask me how my day was? To have my meal on the table. Is it?' Glancing at me now, he shakes his head, 'You should put some ice on that before it swells.'

Entering the kitchen, I switch on the oven, and then reach into the freezer for an ice pack – I do need to reduce the chance of swelling, he's right about that – I can hardly claim that I walked into a cupboard door now can I if bruising does appear.

How am I supposed to work out what he means when he twists things? How am I supposed to know what he's thinking when he doesn't think like a rational human being?

I provoke him?

What a joke!

I'm supposed to ask him how his day was? How about he asks me? Then I can tell him all about the utter pointlessness of my life – the day-to-day fear that I suffer in this house that I used to call my sanctuary.

How was your day, Jade?

It was fine thank you – tea's ready.

September has arrived, but my chance of escape has once again passed me by. Not because Eric has unknowingly prevented it, though he has been working from home a lot lately – which hasn't helped my escape plan, and not because my legs have betrayed me – but because I have the flu!

How can my body do this to me?

I am so utterly drained; my head feels like it's been shoved into a vice and my body crumpled beneath a steam roller. I just do not have the strength to move from my bed.

Eric absolutely forbids me to be anywhere else in the house and has quarantined me to the bedroom. The only concern that he has shown, is to dump soup and hot drinks on my bedside table and beat a hasty retreat. He does not speak to me; he does not comfort me; he does not care.

My parents and Heidi call around to visit me three days into my bed rest – or prison time, whichever you prefer to call it, and Eric really does try his hardest to stop them from entering, but mum, stubborn as always is having none of it. 'We've all had the flu jab, so I don't think

115

there's anything to worry about on that count.' Mum says, 'through there is she?'

'Erm… Jade is in the spare bedroom.' Eric mumbles, 'just on the left there.'

'Why on earth is she in the spare bedroom?' mum snaps, confused, 'that's hardly comforting is it, being shoved out of the way.'

'It was *her* idea.' Eric argues, 'to save me from catching the flu also.'

'Well, that's just silly – if anybody should move bedrooms it should be you. You only need to sleep in there, Jade needs to convalesce. I would have thought you of all people would have understood that after everything she's been through. Honestly, Eric, that is so disappointing of you.'

'Hardly surprising though, hey Eric?' Heidi jibes.

I'm cringing inwardly at the rage I know will be building up inside of Eric, and the punishment that I know I will be at the receiving end of when they all leave. Quickly rubbing foundation and blusher onto my face, I try my best to cover the slight bruising on my cheek.

'Why is it not surprising?' Dad asks, clearly confused.

'A private joke.' Eric laughs, 'It's nothing really.'

'Doesn't sound very amusing.' Dad continues, not at all

impressed with anything that is happening around him. 'Through here you say?' he asks Eric, as the door to the bedroom is pushed open and they all enter with big smiles on their faces – well, all but my husband.

'*You* don't have to stay.' Heidi glares at Eric, 'I'm sure you have plenty to be getting on with, don't let us keep you.'

I don't make eye contact with Eric. I know that his being dismissed by Heidi will not have gone down well with him at all, and I know that I will hear all about it later. As much as I love my parents, and as much as I love Heidi, they would have helped me more by staying away. 'Oh, Jade love.' Mum soothes as she plumps up my pillow, 'how are you feeling?'

'Better than she looks, I hope.' Laughs Heidi, 'You look like shit.'

Laughing, I throw a dirty sock at her and giggle as she jumps away from it, '*I* have the flu, what's your excuse?'

'Now now girls.' Dad referees, 'don't make me ground you both.'

I'm already grounded, dad.

'Really though, is *he* looking after you properly?' Heidi asks, not caring to lower her voice. 'Because you can always come and stay with me.'

117

'You have a one-bedroom apartment.' I laugh, 'where are you going to put me? On the balcony?'

'You can have my bed; I'll take the floor.' She responds in all seriousness. 'Just say the word and it's done.'

'Is there something that we need to be made aware of here?' Mum demands to know, 'Just what aren't you girls telling us?'

'It's nothing, mum.' I soothe, 'Just Heidi playing mother hen.'

'Really Jade? Really?' Heidi snaps, 'I know what...'

'Tea anybody?' Eric asks as he shoves his head around the bedroom door. I don't know how much he heard of our conversation but knowing Eric it will have been every word. He's probably had his ear pressed up to the door this entire time. 'Coffee?'

'I could go for a coffee.' Dad replies, offering to help him, 'We can leave the women to their girlie talk then.'

Out manoeuvred once more, Eric has no choice but to go back into the kitchen with my dad. He can't very well tell dad to make the drinks now can he, while he hangs around for girl talk.

Now would be the perfect opportunity to tell Heidi and my mum exactly what has been going on. But Eric is temperamental, and I cannot predict his response to being challenged by my parents and overprotective best friend. I just need to ride this out. I just need to be patient. One day they will know everything. I will sit them all down and tell them the full story – but today is not that day.

'Did I tell you that Sylvia is getting married?' Mum coos, 'This coming Saturday. I mean it's a bit fast if you ask me, but each to their own.'

I don't have a clue who Sylvia is - it's like when old people read the obituaries and exclaim loudly that Harold Barnaby has died – *ooh he was only ninety-six* – you don't know them either, but you say nothing, just nod sadly.

I'm grateful that mum has steered us away unknowingly from my wellbeing, despite Heidi glaring at me from the end of the bed, I nod, and I smile where required, happy that we have moved onto safer ground – even though Sylvia's upcoming nuptials are a mystery to me.

'I hope you don't catch my cold and pass it on to the bride.' I shiver, 'this one has totally wiped me out.'

'You are made of stronger stuff than that, young lady.' Mum soothes, 'I'll never forget the day that Eric called and told your father that you were in the hospital – I feared the worst – I think we all did. But look at you now! We are so proud of you, for everything that you have overcome.

119

So I don't think a silly little cold is going to stop you, is it.'

Sneezing, I blow my nose and wince at how sore my skin is, 'nothing can stop me, mum. Nothing.' If only she knew that I meant it in ways that are so much more than this sickness.

'That's the spirit!'

Returning with the drinks, Eric is not so easily dismissed this time around, and as he hangs around at the end of the bed, I can feel Heidi's frustration mounting. She knows that I won't admit to anything, and it annoys and upsets her. She just wants to help and cannot understand why I won't allow her to, 'I'm gonna get off Jade.' She murmurs, no longer able to bear being in the same room as my husband, 'let you get some rest.'

'We should really do the same, Evelyn.' Dad agrees, 'Let her get some sleep.'

'But I haven't drunk my tea.' Mum complains theatrically.

'I'll make you a fresh one at home.' Dad promises with a smile, 'let's leave Jade to rest.'

I tell them not to kiss me goodbye, as I don't want to be responsible for any of them picking up my germs, and as Eric ushers them to the front door I hear my mum telling him to make sure I am moved back into the master bedroom and that he looks after me properly. Eric does not take orders well, and as the front door slams shut and he looms in the doorway, I know that I am to be punished for having people care for me.

This it would seem is the true price of being loved.

The flu has finally run its course after just over a week and a half, so feeling much better now, I ask Eric if it would be possible for us to go out for a few hours. Just up the pier and back, maybe grab a bag of fish and chips, and watch the boats.

He laughs.

'And why the hell would I want to do that?'

'Because it would be a nice thing to do.' I respond, bravely. 'I haven't been outside once since I came home – the doctor said that I should get plenty of fresh air.'

'Haven't been out once? What do you call the wasted trips to the physio centre then? Don't make out that I have neglected you, Jade.'

'I'm not.' I apologise, 'it's just the physio centre was hardly a trip out, was it?'

'What you're really saying here is that it wasn't good enough for you – not acceptable for Lady Jade!'

'That's not what I'm saying at all.' I sigh. 'I just thought it might be nice if we spent some time outside of this house, just a few hours to get some fresh air, a change of scenery.'

'Let's get one thing straight.' He barks, putting his face as close to mine as he can get it, 'I'm not taking you outside Jade. Not in *that thing*! Do you have any idea how humiliating it is for me that you can't walk, that you're a cripple? Do you think I want people looking at me with sympathy in their eyes because I got lumbered with a disabled wife? No Jade. If you want to go out, then you better start walking!'

'You know that I can't' I sob, 'I wish that I could. But people won't be thinking that about you Eric, they won't be looking at you that way. If anything, they will feel sorry for me for being temporarily disabled.'

'You *want* people to stare at you?' he demands, 'why? You should be embarrassed too.'

'But I'm not embarrassed. I survived being hit by a car – that's nothing to be ashamed of.'

'Well, I'm ashamed of it. I'm ashamed of you!'

'That's a cruel thing to say.' I whisper, 'You should just be glad that I'm alive.'

Laughing, he begins to push my chair back towards to spare bedroom, 'Glad you're alive? My crippled wife that

122

can't even get pregnant – oh yeah, I should definitely count my blessings.' Tipping me from the wheelchair and onto the floor, he nudges my legs with the tip of his boot, 'you want out then you better start walking. Go on. Walk!'

'But I…'

'Come on! You want this – so get up!'

'Eric, I can't.' I sob.

'You're not even trying! Here, let me help.' Grabbing my arms, he yanks me from the floor so that I am pressed against his chest, leaving my feet dangling in the air. Feet that I dare not move, even though I know what is coming.

'If I drop you now, will you fall? Or, will your legs save you?' he sneers, 'shall we see?'

'I will fall Eric!' I cry out, as he crushes me against his body, 'Just stop, please!'

'Fight or flight Jade?' he laughs as his arms release me from his vice-like grip.

My brain knows that I should stop myself from falling, my natural instincts are to brace myself, but I am doomed if I do, so, I let myself drop. Screaming as my ankle twists beneath me. Clenching my fists, I try my hardest to hold back the overwhelming need to pull my ankle towards me, to rub it better.

'Flight then.' He grins, kneeling before me, 'oh silly Jade.'

He soothes, 'did you go and hurt yourself? Let me see?'

'No.' I yelp, 'please don't touch it.'

Grabbing my ankle he rests it upon his knee and without warning squeezes it.

'Does that hurt?' He laughs as the pain takes my breath away, 'poor baby.'

'Please stop Eric. You've had your fun, okay.'

'You think this is fun for me? You think living like this, with you, is fun for me?'

'Then let me go.' I plead, 'Just let me go.'

'Never Jade.' He snarls, pushing my throbbing foot away from him in disgust, 'Never!'

Taking a deep breath, and brushing away the tears that I could not stop even if I wanted to, I reach out to him and touch his cheek, 'You don't love me, Eric, so why don't we just end this now and you can be with someone that you do love? Doesn't that make more sense than *this*?'

'You seem to think that you have an opinion in this marriage Jade, and I'm not at all sure why. I'm sure that I just made it perfectly clear that I would not let you go. Did you not understand that? Do you need me to speak more slowly?'

'I just…'

'You know, it looks to me like you don't want to go out

after all.'

'No.' I mutter, 'I don't suppose I do.'

'Don't ever ask me again to degrade myself for you and your gimpy legs! And don't ever mention leaving me again! We are married Jade, and you *will* learn how to be a proper wife!'

'I'm sorry, I just thought that we might have a nice time. But you don't seem to enjoy being around me, so maybe...'

'A *nice time*? Pushing you about in a wheelchair?

'I can't help any of this Eric, you know I can't.'

'If you can get your deformed body to work, then I will take you out – so walk! Walk right now!'

'I can't.' I whimper, too afraid to move even one inch.

'Then you stay exactly where you are!'

I will walk Eric, but I'll be dammed if I'll walk for you!

Halloween.

God, I used to love Halloween. Fancy dress nights at *The Dirty Rabbit,* prizes for best costume (*I never won*) – random concoctions made up by Barry the bar manager – and aptly named '*Witches Brew*' or '*Witches Piss*' as we referred to it, dancing the *Time Warp*, and *Michael*

125

Jacksons Thriller, staying up way past the witching hour, before eventually falling into bed still fully made up as whatever gruesome character we had chosen to be.

Yes. I miss those Halloween nights.

But this Halloween night? Well, this Halloween night is different – because Eric is already spoiling for a fight, and you can just guess where that will end up.

'I'm going to have to turn off the lights if those bleedin' kids don't stop knocking!' he fumes, as I place his meal before him on the dining table, 'can't they take a hint?!'

'It's Trick or Treat night, they'll be knocking on all of the doors along here.' I smile, nervously. 'I think we have some sweets in, why don't I hand some out?'

'What and have them tell their mates to come as well? Don't be so bloody stupid!

'It's just harmless fun, Eric.' I murmur. 'They don't mean to annoy you.'

'Do you know what does annoy me, Jade?' he growls, 'This shit!' Throwing the plate of food across the room he reaches across the table and grabs my throat, 'I ask you, nicely, for a simple meal, something that won't give me heartburn, and what do you serve me, *wife*?! Curry! A goddam curry! Are you trying to kill me?'

'But you like Curry, and really it's only a Korma, you

126

should be fine.'

I don't immediately see the outstretched hand that is flying through the air towards me, I also don't immediately react until the crack of his palm against my cheek thunders around the kitchen. Lifting my arms to cover my face, I shield my head as much as I can as I know that the blows will not stop until he has made me bleed.

Grabbing my hair, he pulls me from the wheelchair and looms over me. I know what is coming, and as I close my eyes in defeat, he grabs my jaw and pulls me towards his face, leaving me with no choice but to look at him, to really see him for the monster that he is.

'I should be fine, eh, Jade? Do *you* feel fine?'

'No, I…'

Pushing my head away from him, he lines up to strike me once again, and as his foot strikes my ribs with sickening accuracy, pain explodes across my trembling body.

'Eric please!' I scream, 'Stop! Please god, stop!'

'God?' he smirks, 'God can't help you!'

Pushing myself up onto my elbows I begin to slowly drag myself away from him, still adamant that he does not see that my legs are near on fully recovered now, though I know that I should run, I cannot.

'Where are you going cripple?' he laughs, as my back makes contact with the kitchen units, 'Surely you can't be thinking of *running* away from your husband? Oh yeah, you can't run, can you, cripple!'

The air positively crackles with the rage and violence being emitted from my husband, as he drags me once more into the middle of the kitchen floor.

'You will obey me, *wife*!'

'Eric, please?' I whimper, as he climbs on top of me, his weight suffocating, and repulsive. 'Please don't do this.'

'You need to learn your place. Don't you think that you need to learn that?'

'I do. I do.' I nod, petrified now at what is coming next, 'I will learn, I promise I will. Just please, don't do this.'

'Do what Jade?' he spits, 'come on, you can say the word – what don't you want me to do?'

'I... please don't force me to... to... have... se...sex, please.' I beg.

'Sex?' he howls, as he pulls my dress up around my waist, 'Sex? Christ, you are pathetic! 'I'm going to *fuck* you Jade; I'm going to *fuck* you until you know your place! Sex! What a joke!'

'Please...'

'Oh, you want it now. Well, why didn't you say so.'

Closing my eyes, I try my hardest to take my mind elsewhere, to think of my new life, my future – but I know that that is only possible if I make it through the night. Because it won't stop here – he will drag me into the bedroom next and start all over again – he will keep on going no matter how I beg and plead with him to stop – he will keep on going until he's either too exhausted to continue or until he feels that I now understand my place – it will be the first one, it's always the first one.

I wake in pain. My jaw hurts, I have a pounding headache, and my ribs feel like they have been crushed. I have taken some terrible beatings from Eric since we have been together, our wedding night was a spectacular example, but last night – last night I thought I was going to die. And I welcomed it. I welcomed the release of death. I prayed for it.

As expected, the abuse did not end until the early hours of the morning. Eric would sleep between attacking and raping me, only to awaken, refreshed and ready for the next round. I had dared not sleep. I had considered running to the kitchen as he slept to grab the kitchen knife, I had imagined cutting his throat or stabbing in him his cold black heart – but I had dared not move.

I'm sure people would understand, wouldn't they?

If I killed him? They would say that I did the right thing. That I was pushed to it.

But then, they might ask why I stayed?

Why didn't I flee? And for that, I have no solid response – no answer that would make sense to those people, because in truth, it doesn't really make sense to me.

I was frightened that he would hurt my friends.

I was frightened that he would hurt my parents.

I was frightened that if I failed, he would kill me.

They would not understand those reasons, those people that have perfectly normal marriages. Those people that only argue with their spouse over whose turn it is to wash up or do the laundry, toilet seat up or down, loo roll facing in or out.

No. They would not understand.

They would pry into my life, unravelling every little thing that I've ever done, ever said. They would find pictures of me online, drunk, having fun, and say that I was wild – he had his hands full with me. They would drag my life, my friends' lives, and my parents' lives through the mud because nobody would stay if it was that bad – surely! I must be exaggerating, lying – after all, Eric Sawyer was a well-liked businessman, and I was just a lowly shop

130

assistant.

I was making the whole thing up!

I would be sent to prison, for a very long time – and even that would be better than the life that I lead now, which is no life at all – but still, I could not kill him. He deserves it, but I cannot do it.

It has been six months since I came home, six months of torment, and come hell or high water I am leaving this house - today!

'**I**'ll be at a conference for two days; do you think you can manage by yourself for that long?' Eric asks me with a smirk.

I know that he isn't asking over concern for my wellbeing, he's just saying it to be an arsehole. But two days at a make-believe conference works perfectly for me. I know of course that he's off visiting one of his many girlfriends, and I do wonder if he treats them as appallingly as he treats me – I bet he doesn't.

'I'll be fine.' I mumble, my jaw still paining me when I speak, 'I have food in and…'

'Great. I'll see you in two days.' Shrugging into his jacket he makes for the door, only to pause and look over his shoulder, 'oh and Jade? Don't do anything stupid while

I'm gone. I'd hate for that lesson to have to be re-taught.'

Oh, I'll just bet you'd hate it.

'I won't.'

'I haven't scheduled any visitors for you either, so you might as well take this time to work on your attitude. I've bought you some books to read, I think they'll be beneficial.'

'Books? What kind of books?'

'Over there. You should have enough time to get them finished before I'm back. It's not like you do anything else all day, is it.'

Looking across to where he is pointing, I see the books that he has ever so carefully picked out for me:

How to maintain a perfect home.

How to please your man.

How to have a more fulfilling sex life.

Discover your inner domestic goddess.

So, books that benefit him then.

'That's very thoughtful of you.' I smile, 'I will definitely start reading them today.'

'Make sure you do. Especially that second one!'

As he slams the door behind him, I take the books and slowly begin to rip out each page. *Screw you, Eric!*

Wheeling myself across to the window I watch as he

disappears and his whistling fades away – knowing that I will wait just a little longer to ensure that he really has gone. I will put a movie on, any old thing will do, just something to count down the time until I can leave. Eric would not stand about outside in the freezing cold October wind for ninety minutes just to catch me out – so if he hasn't made an appearance by the end of the film, then I am good to go. I feel jittery. I feel as though I am doing something terrible. When all I am really doing is saving my life.

The film, *Ace Ventura Pet Detective* is ridiculous, but amusing enough to calm my nerves, that by the time the credits roll, I can calmy retrieve my suitcase and open the front door.

Cold fresh air whips around my face for the first time in months and I lap it up. The sting of the bitterly cold wind against my cheeks, the sounds of seagulls and children laughing, the smell of fish and chips – this is what freedom smells and sounds like - Like simple things.

My legs feel a little shaky, partly because they are not yet fully recovered, and partly because the beating that I took last night really knocked the wind out of me. But as I said before, if I must crawl, then I will.

The one hundred and ninety-nine steps are going to

take a massive toll on my legs, but if I pace myself, I know that I can make it.

Walking steadily, I pass the houses of my neighbours, praying that none of them sees me, that none of them has anything to report back to Eric should he ask. The steps are not far now, and as I pull my coat and scarf closer around my face to keep the chilly breeze out, I begin to feel a tiny surge of excitement building deep within my chest.

The shops are busy despite the cold weather, and I find myself dodging shoppers, laden with bags of seaside goodies, sticks of rock and souvenirs, again totally oblivious to my plight.

When I finally reach the bottom of the steps, I grab the handrail with one unsteady hand as I grip my suitcase tightly in the other, unsure now if my trembling legs will take me all the way to the top. My body aches from the force of Eric's anger last night, and the cold north wind bites deep into my bones, further paining my already throbbing jaw. I know that I need to get up these steps, I know that this is the only way that I can be free, but these one hundred and ninety-nine steps might as well as be a mountain!

I can feel tears burning the backs of my eyes as I

consider the mammoth task ahead of me, I knew it wouldn't be easy, but right now it feels damn near impossible. I can't even see the top of the steps from where I am, so steep is the climb. Would I be willing to admit defeat without even trying? Could I face walking back through my front door, resigned to a life of misery?

'You alright there lovey?' a deep, solemn voice asks from behind me, interrupting my gloomy thoughts. 'Bit of a bugger these stairs, aren't they? You going up or just reached the bottom?'

Great, just what I need! Please don't be kind to me old man, I can't handle my own tears right now. If I start, I may never stop.

'Oh, going up.' I grimace, 'Well, hoping to anyway.'

'They don't get any easier.' He chuckles, pulling his hat further down onto his head, 'I remember when I could run right to the top without stopping, but I was a lot fitter then, and around about thirty years younger.'

Laughing despite my current predicament, I smile warmly at the old man, 'you don't fancy offering a girl a piggyback, do you?'

'Lass, if my knees could take it, and again if I were thirty years younger, I would certainly take you up on that offer.' He winks, 'you just pace yourself, there's no rush.'

Oh, but there is – there really is.

'Thanks.' I smile, 'I suppose I better start, otherwise I'll be here all night.'

'Are you okay though?' he asks again, 'other than the thought of that climb?'

'I will be.'

'You could always get a taxi you know.' He says, with a nod in the direction of the town centre, 'why make things difficult if you don't have to.'

'Because then there wouldn't be a sense of achievement at the end of it?' I respond, sounding a lot more like the Jade of old. 'Why pass up a challenge?'

'Why indeed. Just don't overdo it okay – use the rest benches, take a breather, take your time.'

I wish I had time.

As the old man waves a cheery goodbye, I take the first official step towards my new life. My legs feel unsteady as I pull myself up onto the next one, and then the next, each one more gruelling than the last, the suitcase banging heavily against my knees as I move.

Only one hundred and ninety-five to go.

What would normally take a few minutes has in fact taken me thirty-six. I have stopped more than I have walked, I have fought back tears every time my legs have buckled, and I have smiled bravely at the four individuals that stopped to ask if I needed help.

No matter the pain that my legs are no in, no matter the heaving of my chest as I try desperately to drag oxygen into my lungs, and no matter the pounding in my head – I have made it to the top. Somehow, I have made it.

I do have another trek ahead, however, this time in the form of a dirt path that will lead me directly up to the car park. The walk is tough, and my legs are desperate to stop and rest, but if I do, then I fear I may not start again. Thankfully the grass at either side of the dirt track is overgrown and unruly, which unlike the steps will give me some sort of cover from prying eyes - be those the eyes of strangers, or the eyes of somebody that Eric may know.

Gulping down water, I press on, only stopping once to pet a horse that has his nose stuck over the fence to my right - an excuse to stop? Probably. I always thought that I was fit, and maybe I was before the accident, but now I am puffing and panting like a heavy smoker – I need to concentrate massively on my health and fitness once I'm settled.

At the end of the dirt track now, I pass through the kissing gate and there it is - the little blue car – it is parked exactly where the salesman said that it would be.

I cry now.

Tears of gratitude, tears of relief, tears of pain and tears of complete and utter joy. I am literally just a few steps away from freedom!

The car itself doesn't look exactly like the photographs online – I certainly hadn't seen quite so many scratches and dents when I glanced at the images. But scratches won't prevent me from driving the vehicle, and I did want something quick with no questions asked, so I suppose you get what you pay for.

Reaching beneath the wheel arch I feel urgently for the keys that I requested be taped there, gasping aloud as my fingers brush the cold plastic of the key fob, feeling instantly relieved that they have not fallen off and been kicked accidentally into the grass verge, away from view, upending my plans.

Clicking the fob, I begin to panic as nothing happens. No lights flash, and no doors click open. Nothing. *Breathe Jade*, I think to myself as I instead flick out the key and insert it into the lock – it's just a duff fob – the batteries have probably died, and I'm sure the freezing cold wind up here hasn't helped matters.

The car smells of stale cigarettes and sweat, but to me,

it smells almost sweet – like victory, and as I settle inside, throwing the suitcase onto the back seat, I turn the engine on and sigh in relief, this is it! I'm finally leaving! My triumph however is short-lived as I press down on the accelerator, only for the car to lurch forward and stop again just as suddenly, as a metallic grinding sound echoes throughout the vehicle, and the lights on the dashboard fade away to darkness. Turning the key once more I beg the car to start, but it remains unmoving. Slamming my hands down on the steering wheel, I scream.

I scream as loud as my lungs will allow - the car is dead. Whatever the reason may be for this mechanical failure I have no way in which to solve the problem, and as the car park stands deserted, I have nobody that I can ask for help. I said that I didn't want to be blindsided, but despite my careful and thorough planning, I have been.

Climbing wearily now from the car, I find that I do not even have it in me to kick the bloody thing. My suitcase feels heavier than before now, though I know that that isn't possible – maybe it isn't the suitcase at all – maybe it's just my body getting ready to power down, unable to deal with any more of this shit.

I climbed the steps for nothing.

I walked the dirt path for nothing.

I am defeated before I even get started.

Falling to my knees beside the car that has let me down in the most monumental of ways, I sob. Not for the steps, not for the walk and not for the stinky scratch-laden car – but because I feel weary. Because I feel like giving up and just going home. Because I failed.

What can I do now? My entire being hurts – I don't think I have anything left in me.

Popping open my suitcase I pull out another bottle of water and a packet of painkillers. I could just take the lot, I could just end it all right here, right now. But I'm not that person, I couldn't bear the thought of somebody finding me like that, and I don't think six Ibuprofen will do that much harm anyway. Swallowing down two pills I spot my MP3 player poking out from one of my trainers, pulling it out I slowly unravel the earphone cable and pop the buds into my ears. Heidi has always said that music has gotten her through some dark times, and I never really understood what she meant – but I am prepared to try anything right now.

As the music of the first track begins to play, I feel almost as though the MP3 player knows, almost as if it is aware that I need these particular words, this particular song to pick myself back up, dust myself off and keep moving. So, I push the volume button determinedly until it's at the highest setting and I let Britney Spears, *Stronger*, wash over me.

'Hush, just stop
There's nothing you can do or say, baby
I've had enough
I'm not your property as from today, baby
You might think that I won't make it on my own

But now I'm stronger than yesterday
Now it's nothing but my way
My loneliness ain't killing me no more
I, I'm stronger'

Feeling empowered now, I shakily drag myself from the damp car park floor and re-assess my situation. Yes, I should have considered that something could potentially go wrong with the car. I shouldn't have put all of my faith into a blind internet sale.

And yes, I should have factored in a backup plan, should anything go wrong. But I felt so confident that the car was the answer – I was wrong.

Now I need an alternative, and time is not currently on my side. The longer I stay still, the stronger the chances are that somebody will spot me.

Thinking back to the old man, and his idea of hailing a taxi, I decide the only way forward now is to make my way back into the centre of town and head immediately for the bus station. I know that the walk would normally take around fifteen minutes, but this is not a normal situation. My legs are burning and feel like they could buckle at any moment, so I need to act fast and get back down those steps.

The dirt track is thankfully much easier to navigate now that I am going downhill, but the steps themselves are hazardous. As they are shallow and quite close together you would think it would make my life easier, but it does not. It means that my steps must be more carefully considered, as there isn't much room at all for miscalculations and I can't risk a tumble.

I have quite the walk ahead of me, and as I limp, slowly and precisely to the bottom of the shiny smooth steps I find myself gasping for breath, but unable to rest. I cannot risk even a few moments to catch my breath, not this close to home.

Passing the *Whitby Jet Store*, I know that this is the area where I must remain extra vigilant, as the quickest route to the bus stop will take me directly in front of the *White Horse & Griffin* pub – Eric's pub! It is here that I could potentially be spotted by any number of Eric's drinking buddies, not to mention Eric himself, if the *conference* as I believe it to be is a total work of fiction. I should have worn a disguise I chuckle sadly to myself as I push my way in between the shoppers, placing a human shield between myself and the pub windows. I dare not even risk a glance at the building as I slowly edge my way past, grateful for the family of six that I have managed to attach myself to – just one glance could ruin everything that I have been through to get here, just one glance could end me.

The cobblestone road that I am currently on is where Heidi saw me that fateful Christmas, it is the one that I ran down as though the demons of hell were chasing me, and it is the one that leads me over the swing bridge and onto Quay Road where I was knocked down by that poor driver just going about his or her daily business.

I have thought many times about that driver. How they must have felt that day, how they must feel now. It must be terrible to know that you have hit somebody with your car, even though you weren't at all to blame. I wish that I could apologise to them, say that they have nothing at all to feel bad about, but I have no way of doing such a thing, and so I must put it behind me, as I hope they will do one day.

'Jade?' a man's voice hollers from behind me, 'Jade, is that you?'

I do not stop. I do not acknowledge that I have heard anything. *What is it with this bloody street?!* Blood pumps heavily through my veins now as my heart beats faster and sweat begins to form on my face and neck. I do not recognise the voice, but clearly, the person recognises me. 'Jade!' He continues to yell, 'Does Eric know that you are up and about? Jade?'

I knew it.

I just knew that one of Eric's spies would see me, he does seem to have a lot of them. I risk a slight glance across my shoulder and see that a man is trying to push his way through the crowds that are gathering by the swing bridge, and I know that it must be about to open. I need to get across that bridge before the mystery man catches up with me!

Channelling all of the energy reserves that I have left, I make a run for it, well aware that this course of action is exactly what put me in the hospital last time, but just like last time, I have no choice.

The bridge is part way open now as I throw myself up and onto it, dragging my suitcase behind me. Shouts of shock and disbelief follow in my wake as I scramble up and struggle to my feet, wincing at the cut that has opened on my kneecap.

'Jade! Jesus Christ!'

'What the hell are you doing?'

'Get down from there right now!'

'She'll never make it! The boat is coming!'

But I do make it, and as I safely reach the other side, I look back across the bridge to see the man that had chased me is now on his mobile phone. I need to leave. Now!

'That was a really stupid thing to do!' a woman snaps at me, as I limp past her, my poor legs almost at breaking point. 'Bloody idiot!'

I don't bother to respond. What would be the point? They have no idea what I have been through, what it took for me to make that leap, and I see no reason to justify my actions to a total stranger. I risked my life to save it, and that is all that matters.

I know that if Eric's friend had caught up with me, he would never have let me leave and that the punishment I would have received for such a betrayal would probably have resulted in my death this time.

I don't have long before the swing bridge is closed again, allowing people to cross, safely, and I am sure that

Eric will have ordered his spy to hunt me down. My body hurts in every place that it is possible to feel pain, but I push myself for hopefully the last time up Station Road and into the bus station.

I know what I must look like. Limping, sweating, my hair plastered to my head, my suitcase dragging on the floor – but I don't care. I would walk through here naked if it meant I could find a bus to take me away from all of this madness.

'Excuse me?' I ask the ticket attendant in the tiny booth before me, my words coming out rapidly and jagged, 'Are any buses leaving now? Like, right now?'

'Where to?' she asks, disinterested in the mess of a woman before her.

'It doesn't matter.' I respond, impatiently as I look again over my shoulder, 'to anywhere.'

'Devil chasing you, is he?'

'Is there a bus leaving or not?!' I snap, finally reaching boiling point for what has already been a really shitty day.

'Okay, okay. No need to bite my head off. There's a bus leaving for Scarborough in eighteen minutes, is that quick enough for you?'

'Not really, no. Is there anything else?'

Eighteen minutes? He could easily catch up with me in

eighteen minutes.

'Leeds, in two minutes, but I doubt you'll make it, the state that you're in.'

'Look.' I begin with a sob, 'I'm running away from my husband, he's a mean bastard that wants to hurt me, well, as you can probably tell he's already hurt me, so please, if there is any way at all that I can get on that Leeds bus I would be eternally grateful.'

I hadn't meant to say any of that. I hadn't meant to tell anybody what was happening to me, I hadn't wanted any witnesses. But I've gone and done it now.

Eyeballing me and my small, battered suitcase, she smiles sadly, 'well, why didn't you say so? Men, eh? Waste of bleedin' space! You want on that bus girl, you got it!'

'There's another thing.' I whisper, 'One of his friends is chasing me, I don't think I have long.'

'Oh, is that so. Well, don't you worry yourself about that.' Picking up her radio she presses the button down and begins to speak, her tone authoritative and not to be argued with. 'Roger, we have a young lady here that needs to be on that Leeds bus, I'm bringing her down now.'

'But…'

'It isn't open for discussion.' She growls, 'oh and Roger, send security to the booth, we have a potential code blue.'

147

Turning to face me, she takes the suitcase from my shaking hands and motions for me to turn right.

'I'm sorry that I snapped at you.' I sob, 'it' hasn't been a great day. Well, it hasn't been a great few years actually.'

'I know exactly where you're coming from.' She smiles, 'and it will get better, believe me, it will.'

'You do?' I ask, surprised that the strong woman before me could ever have suffered as I have.

'Oh yeah! Ten years, eleven days, and nine hours of understanding where you're coming from! It took everything I had to walk out of that door and start a new life. You can too you know. Just don't be fooled into thinking he's changed. If he tells you that he has, do not under any circumstance believe him. Monsters can't change.'

'I won't. I know that he'll never change – he's evil.'

'Do you have someplace in mind to stay when you get to Leeds?' she asks, as she passes my suitcase to the driver for loading, 'someone that you can call?'

'I'll probably just find a hotel for tonight and work things out in the morning. I just need one good night's sleep before I make any decisions.'

'Girl, you look like you need a week's worth of sleep.' She smiles. Handing me a slip of paper with her name and telephone number on it, she tells me to call her if I need to talk, 'you're not alone, you know.'

Stepping up onto the bus, I wave wearily to my new friend and settle down into the cushioned seats. I know that I won't call her. Not because I don't want to, but because she is now a witness to where I am heading, and I can't put her in danger by telling her more than she needs to know. Ignoring the blatant stares from my fellow travellers, no doubt wondering why I am so sweaty and bedraggled, I close my eyes and concentrate only on the vibrations of the bus as they rattle through my broken body.

I am free.

PART THREE

NEW BEGINNINGS...

'Good morning, Peyton, lovely day, isn't it? Are you heading over to the village hall?'

'I sure am. Do you want me to let Dorothy know that you'll be over shortly to help with the bunting?'

'Oh, now now, Miss Grey. Don't you be giving me that wink, you know as well as I do that it won't just stop with bunting! No, no, I plan to finish these last few deliveries and have myself a well-earned pint. Bunting indeed!'

'So, I'm going to hazard a guess, Alf, that you'd prefer it if I didn't mention that I'd seen you?'

'Well don't be getting me wrong, I love that wife of mine dearly – but bunting is women's business, it's no place for a man. All those frills and lacey things – ooh, it makes my blood run cold just thinking about it.'

'Then your secret is safe with me.'

'I knew I had an ally in you, Miss Grey, it's been a pleasure from the moment you arrived.'

'I think it's been more like a secret society since I arrived Alf, and you and I are the only members.'

Laughing, Alf, the friendliest postman in Bardsey, tips his cap and with a wink and a skip, heads in the opposite direction of his beloved wife Dorothy – who would scowl just a little if she knew that dear old Alf planned to drink the day away and play dominos.

Peyton Grey.

It's taking some getting used to, and even after three years, I don't automatically turn around if someone calls my name. My very new, very different, very safe name.

That final day in Whitby, where I ran as though the demons of hell were chasing me, is still fresh in my mind. I don't think the memory of the fear that buzzed through my body will ever truly leave me. It may fade, a little, but it will never be gone.

I had sat on the bus both relieved and terrified.

Relieved that I had made it, relieved that a friendly face was there to help me in my moment of need, and relieved that I was one more step closer to escaping my abuser.

But, terrified that he would find me. That his friend, the one that had chased me, would have called Eric, and that no amount of security would prevent him from dragging me from the bus. Terrified with each stop that we made that he would be there, waiting to board, his eyes boring into mine, telling me without words that I would pay for this betrayal. When I arrived in Leeds City Centre I felt instantly lost. I had panicked and pushed my way through the throng of travellers boarding and alighting, and had taken a moment, in a quiet corner just to catch my breath. I had no clue where anything was or where I planned to go,

I only knew that I needed to get as far away from the bus station as possible. I had been surprised at the number of drunken revellers out so early but knew I could hide amongst them if need be. Crowds were my friend right now.

Crowds had served me well in Whitby, and I knew that Leeds would be no different.

Walking through the town centre I had stumbled upon a small, unassuming bed and breakfast, the kind of place that Eric would instantly disregard, and had booked myself in under the name of *Annie Rhodes* and paid in cash. Sure, there were a few peculiar guests, and some who were most certainly *working*, but I didn't care. I would take these people over Eric any day!

The receptionist asked me no questions, and I was relieved not to have to lie, to think of something on the spot. She simply handed me my key and shoved her face back into her mobile phone. How I wished at that moment that my life was as simple as how many *likes* I received on my *Instagram* posts. I hoped that her life would stay that way, free, and easy, just like it used to be for me.

After showering in a surprisingly brilliant shower, and calling down to reception for some sandwiches, I knew that I had to admit defeat and call Gordon. I couldn't manage any further on my own. I had no idea where to go, I only had a small amount of cash on me, and I dared not use my bank card. Gordon was my only hope.

I had sworn Gordon to secrecy when we spoke, told him that he must not under any circumstances tell Heidi what was happening, or where I was, that I could not risk putting her in danger, and when he arrived at the bed and breakfast later that night, I had been somewhat overwhelmed to see not only Gordon, but a sobbing Heidi pushing her way frantically towards me.

I had fallen immediately into her arms, my anger at Gordon never even materializing – he knew that I needed my best friend, he knew that even more than I did.

I told them everything.

Naturally, Heidi's first response was to get back into the car, drive like a maniac to Whitby and pummel Eric to death. Gordon had been jangling his keys, eager to join her. But, somehow, I had managed to talk them down.

I didn't want that. Of course, I knew that Eric needed to be punished, but I didn't want my friends being slap bang in the middle of it. Eric is a dangerous man, and even though I know that Gordon can take of himself, I just could not chance how underhanded my husband could be.

So once again they were sworn to secrecy.

They did not know where I was.

They had not heard from me.

It was the only way that I could ensure their safety, I would speak with the police in my own time when I felt more confident, when I felt more like me.

Heidi had wanted to stay with me that night, desperate not to let me out of her sight, but I had assured her that I was fine and that it would be better if she returned home to keep up appearances. If Eric noticed that we were both missing then she would become his number one target. She had laughed and told me she hopes that he does, but I knew deep down that she was scared too.

I was grateful that Heidi had not once said *I told you so*, but I knew she wouldn't, she wasn't like that. But she did tell me so, many times, and I hadn't listened.

I had only spent a few nights in the bed and breakfast before Gordon returned, and in that time, I had plucked up the courage to call my parents and let them know what was happening – well, a watered-down version of what was happening anyway. I would tell them the full story in time, but for now, it was safer for them if they just believed that I no longer loved Eric and needed some head space. The less they knew, the less Eric could play mind games with them.

Mum, had tried her best to talk me around, to tell me that all marriages have rough patches, that it takes work and sacrifice – I hadn't the heart to tell her just how many sacrifices I had already made. I simply explained to her that my mind could not be changed, my decision was final. She had had no choice but to accept that the matter was closed.

Dad was a lot more laid back about the whole thing, saying only that as long as I was happy then that was all that mattered, oh, and that he never really liked Eric anyway. I did chuckle at that I'll admit.

I know that Eric will contact my parents, they will no doubt be the first people he visits, certain that they are hiding me. If my mum and dad just think that it's over, if they don't know the full story, the horrors that went on inside of my sham marriage then they cannot accidentally give anything away.

Gordon had a whole plan of action mapped out for my immediate future, and the first part of it was to take my bank card, and in return give me twenty thousand pounds in cash. He would fly to Spain the following day, and various other countries after that, and draw money out of my account to recoup what he had given me. That way, my card, if traced, would never be in the location that I was.

It would take a while, and a few trips to the ATM to recoup twenty thousand pounds, but Gordon didn't mind – he liked travelling. He also had a huge property portfolio in the EU, which would give him the perfect cover story.

I knew that the money in my account wouldn't last forever and that eventually, I would need to look at other ways to bring money in, and the one that stuck out as the most obvious was the sale of my Whitby home. I was reluctant of course, but I knew with him out there, I could never go back to the home that I loved.

I doubt it would feel like home now anyway.

I did smile though at the thought of the estate agent popping around to do a valuation – christ, Eric would be livid! Estate Agents and for-sale boards are a long way off yet however, I cannot even begin to process that at the moment.

The next part of Gordon's plan was to move me out of the bed and breakfast and into someplace that I could, albeit temporarily, call home. He had a new listing on his books, a sweet little cottage in the village of Bardsey. It had not yet been advertised as one of his properties, and so would not be traceable.

I had tried to negotiate a fair rent for the property, but Gordon would not hear another word spoken of finances.

He simply said that the house was mine, rent-free for as long as I needed it.

Bardsey is lovely.

Situated in the beautiful countryside it is incredibly peaceful and quaint. Castle Gate Cottage has four bedrooms, a lovely long path leading up to a blue door, a sweet little porch and cream shutters on the windows. Inside it is simply just beautiful. The kitchen is open plan, and the living room is cosy and warm with a conservatory coming off of it, which leads to a cute little garden. Upstairs there are four good-sized bedrooms and the bathrooms are bright and fresh. It is the most perfect example of an English country cottage that I have ever seen - it is also pleasantly located just a stone's throw away from the church, village hall, and the oldest pub in England, *The Bingley Arms*.

I love Whitby right down to my bones, and I miss it, oh god do I miss it – but Bardsey is the light shining through all of the darkness that has shadowed me for so many years – Bardsey will light my path back home.

My life is so much simpler now. No extravagancies, no wild nights out at *The Dirty Rabbit*, heading home at stupid o'clock.

I like it.

I do.

But how I miss those nights, the laughter, the fun, the drunken flirting and dancing on tables – I even miss the hangovers!

I miss my life before Eric.

I miss my life.

I do not use social media, not even in my new name, and I try to avoid any photographs that are taken by pretending to be camera shy, because I cannot risk Eric tracking me down.

I don't know if he is looking for me – it has been three years after all – but if I know Eric as well as I believe I do, then he won't have stopped. I have dented his pride, betrayed and humiliated him – his punishment of me is probably all that is fuelling him even now.

Heidi has not seen sight nor sound of him recently, nor have my parents. He stopped calling them just a few months after my disappearance – but to me that means nothing. He is sneaky, and I would not trust him as far as I could throw him.

I've done just about everything that I can to stay out of

the public eye and to not draw attention to myself. No *Facebook, Instagram or Twitter*. No bank account, I do everything in cash, complete name change, and the worst of all, I have cut myself off from my friends and family. I know that I can call Heidi, Gordon and my parents whenever I like, using disposable mobile phones, but it's not the same as seeing them, being with them, touching them. One day I will be able to do all of that, one day I will be Jade Locke once more, but for now?

For now, I must keep myself safe and my family safe.

There is a madman out there who will stop at nothing to destroy me.

Standing in front of the plain but sturdy village hall doors, I smile to myself at the chatter already building behind them. The force of the local gossipmongers already gathering momentum, because the ladies of this sweet little village do love a good dose of scandal. I just hope that I'm never at the centre of it.

What would they think of me if they knew?

That I deserved it?

That I made my bed?

I hope to never find out.

Wincing, I rub my leg, the pain of which still throbs

occasionally, reminding me, not, that I was a victim, but that I am very much a survivor. Even in my weakest moments, when my body nearly gave up on me, I was strong. I was stronger than Eric will ever be.

I should be proud of that, of how far I've come, but sometimes, it's like I never escaped at all

Pushing open the village hall door, I smile at the utter chaos that has overtaken the large room. Alf was right, there is bunting *everywhere*, and a naughty part of me wishes I'd headed to the *Bingley Arms* with him!

The ladies of Bardsey are currently preparing for a village fete, to raise money for a new church roof, and the church in Bardsey – *All Hallows* - is absolutely beautiful. It has been my sanctuary on many a dark day, and despite not having one ounce of religion within me, I have embraced it fully, with an open heart. It seemed only right then that I would give something back to the village that has saved me. 'Good morning.' Hollers Jemima from the back of the hall, 'see that leg is paining you again?' Jemima is the biggest busybody in the village. With her perfectly coiffed blonde hair and talon-like red nails, she does not look anywhere near her sixty years of age, but she's a dedicated curtain twitcher for sure.

'Oh, you know.' I smile, 'it'll settle soon enough.'

'Peyton, dearie.' Grins Dorothy, as she hands me a huge bundle of bunting, 'you didn't happen upon that husband of mine on your way in did you?'

Dumping the bunting onto the table behind me, I open my mouth to lie but am saved at the last moment by Sally – the biggest pot stirrer in Bardsey.

'He'll be in the pub, Dot, you'll not see him again until tea time. Am I right or am I right Clara?'

With a sigh, Dorothy begins to thread more ribbon, through even more bunting, as Clara, our church mouse, shrugs and gets her head back into her work.

Clara is a real sweetie. She doesn't say a lot, but she is always busy. There are no idle hands where Clara is concerned.

'You're right of course.' Chuckles Dorothy, 'and I know that he probably swore you to secrecy young Peyton, so I'll not drag you into his antics any further.'

'Well, I…'

'It's no bother, I know what a scoundrel he is after all these years.'

'Just how long have you been married, Dorothy?' I ask, genuinely interested, as I'd not been so successful in mine – then again, Alf isn't exactly a maniac is he? If the only thing Dorothy has to grumble about in her marriage is Alf playing dominos, then I think she'll be okay.

'Fifty-two years this coming summer. It's some miracle don't you think?'

'Wow! What's your secret? How do you stay with one person for so long?'

'Well, that's simple dearie.' She winks, 'you never go to sleep on an argument, you accept that marriages are hard work, you compromise, you don't grumble too much when he buggers off to the pub to play dominos, and you try to keep things fresh like they were in the younger days – if you catch my meaning.'

'You'll be making the youngster blush Dot.' Laughs Jemima. Heartily, 'We don't *do it* at our age.'

'Well, you might not!' howls Dorothy, 'but my Alf…'

Laughter echoes around the large hall as a burst of fresh air suddenly wafts in from behind us. 'Sorry to interrupt ladies.' A deep voice booms around the large room, 'I have a delivery for you, I think it's garlands.'

All eyes turn to me and I instantly blush. 'Oh, hi Jake.' I mutter, as I quickly busy myself with detangling the bunting that I so carelessly dumped earlier. 'What are you doing here?' I know it's a stupid question as soon as the words leave my mouth. He's just told us why he's here for crying out loud!

'Erm, garlands….' He replies, clearly confused.

'Oh, yeah.' I mumble, blushing again.

'Ooh, I think someone has gone all shy.' Sally laughs, as she nudges me. 'I can feel the heat from your cheeks a mile off.'

Scowling, I hiss at her to shush and avoid all eye contact with Jake.

Now it's not that I don't like him, I honestly do. And it's not because I've sworn off all men forever because I haven't. I just can't bear the thought of our, well, whatever it is, being picked apart before it's even really begun. And I know that the ladies don't mean any harm, it's just a bit of fun - but to me, this is serious business.

Jake is warm and kind, funny and generous - the polar opposite of my husband. But there was a time, even though deep down I doubted it, that I believed Eric to be kind and loving, so I need to be extra careful this time, to ensure that I haven't been sent another lunatic. Cupid has definitely been off his game lately.

'We still on for that drink later?' He asks me, with a smile, totally oblivious to my discomfort. 'Shall I pick you up at seven?'

It feels pleasantly nice to be asked if I want to do something, as opposed to being told what I will and will not do, and I don't think the novelty of that will ever wear off.

I haven't told Jake everything about my past. Not because I'm ashamed to, and not because I fear he will turn away from me – but because I'm just not ready.
I'm not ready for the questions, or the pity that will flash across his face and I'm certainly not ready for the promises that he will inevitably make to never hurt me.
Promises that he will never be able to keep.
I'm simply not ready.

I have of course told him that I was married, well, that I'm technically still married. I have told him that I have left my marriage and skimmed ever so gently over the reason why.
Jake finds Eric's OCD amusing – I decided not to tell him just how sinister his OCD really is, how utterly terrifying. Jake has never invited me back to his home, he always picks me up, despite how close we both live to the pub and the fact that we could just meet there – but it's nice. It's nice to be picked up, to have someone care enough to do that. And although there is a huge part of me that is curious about how Jake lives, I respect his privacy enough not to push him.

Now, naturally, I do feel some concern that there is a

part of Jake's life that I do not know about, and in my darkest moments, when I lay in bed alone, and my mind wanders into shady territory, I convince myself, if only temporarily, that he has secrets, dark, horrifying secrets, secrets that will hurt me.

The few dates that we've had have been lovely. There hasn't been one single thing that has set alarm bells ringing. Surely then he must just be a normal man, right? Even I couldn't be *that* unlucky!

'Seven okay?' Jake asks again, snapping me out of my irrational musings.

'Daydreaming about the boy.' Laughs Sally, nudging me, 'answer the lad, or I'll take your place.'

Smiling, I tell Jake that seven will be perfect, 'shall we just meet there, or…'

'I'll pick you up.' He grins, 'why break the ritual now.'

Ice-cold fear runs through my veins at the mention of rituals, and I have to hold onto the table to steady myself as images flash through my mind one after the other – Eric's all-consuming rituals and the punishment that I would face for not completing them– *'Make sure you are waiting for me in that red lingerie when I get home from the pub, hang your clothes in colour order, arrange the tins this way not that way, close the blinds to the left, make my coffee at this temperature'* – rituals, rituals, RITUALS!

'Oh, my goodness.' Dorothy exclaims, rushing to my side and helping me onto a seat, 'you look like you've just seen a ghost dearie, whatever is the matter?'

'I....I...' I cannot get the words out, and I feel ridiculous for reacting so illogically – it was just a word – just a normal word. The concern on Jake's face is not helping me to feel any less foolish, and I find that I cannot look him in the eye. 'I think you need to go home to bed.' Commands Jemima, 'bath and bed, you must be coming down with something.'

'No... I...'

'No buts young lady. I'm sure that Jake can walk you home, can't you Jake? Make sure you don't have another funny turn on the way.'

'Yeah, yeah, sure.' He mumbles, unsure what to do.

'I'm fine, honestly.' I croak, 'I'm just a little dizzy, it'll pass, and the bunting needs...'

'You never mind the bunting, home, bed, now.'

I can see that I have no choice in the matter, and as I fight to hold back tears, I allow Jake to walk me home, embarrassment burning my cheeks. I cannot look him in the eye as he opens the door for me, making sure that I am inside safely before leaving me to get some rest. I feel so incredibly stupid and I know that I won't sleep, no matter how hard I try to. How could I when it would seem that even though Eric is miles away, he still has power over me? A power that I do not know how to defeat.

Kicking the duvet onto the floor with a huff, I throw my book onto the bedside cabinet and sigh. What the hell is wrong with me? It was a stupid little word, RITUALS! Why have I reacted so idiotically! Jake must think I'm a right fool, not to mention the ladies at the church group. At least they only think I'm *coming down with something*, yeah, a bad case of the husband crazies!

Mentally I don't think I'm at all okay, which is hardly surprising. I've dealt with so much, emotionally and physically, it's no wonder I'm constantly fearing my own shadow.

I wonder if I have some sort of PTSD?

People have that don't they when they've been through something horrendous – do I need help? Professionally? But, isn't it mostly men and women who have seen and heard vile things in wars? Experienced situations that no everyday person would experience?

But, haven't I also experienced that? Haven't I also been

through something that other people only read about in magazines?

I need to be able to get past this. It's destroying everything that so much as hints at bringing me joy!

Grabbing my mobile phone I do a quick internet search for symptoms of PTSD and am not all surprised with the results;

Vivid flashbacks (feeling like the trauma is happening right now)

Intrusive thoughts or images.

Nightmares.

Intense distress at real or symbolic reminders of the trauma.

Physical sensations such as pain, sweating, nausea, or trembling.

I need help.

Standing outside of the therapist's office, I take a deep steadying breath, I don't think that I can do this, I don't think I can physically move my legs to walk up the four steps ahead of me. I certainly don't think I can force words out of my mouth, honest and open words, words that will tell a tale so unbelievable that I fear the therapist will think me dishonest.

What was I thinking coming here.

They make it look so easy on the TV, just lay back on the chaise longue and spill your guts. Casual, no drama. I can't do that.

No. I have made a huge mistake. I'll go home, call them as soon as I get in and apologise for being a timewaster. They'll understand, this must happen all the time.

'Heading in?' A cheery voice sings from behind me, 'I promise we don't bite.'

The lady before me is beautiful. Long dark hair down to her waist, porcelain skin, totally free of makeup, and huge blue eyes.

'We?' I mumble, confused.

'Oh, sorry.' She chuckles, thrusting her hand towards me, 'I'm Maya, the head receptionist here. Are you going in for an appointment?'

'Erm...'

'First time?' She asks with a friendly smile.

'I just, erm... well it's...'

'I totally understand first appointment nerves. But genuinely, we are friendly, it's a very relaxed, laid-back atmosphere. Stella is fantastic, you'll be in good hands. Shall we get you inside?'

I feel railroaded. I can hardly scarper now.

With another deep breath, I follow Maya up the stairs and into the warm and welcoming reception area.

'Can I take a name please?' She asks as she logs onto her computer.

'Peyton.' I smile warily, 'Peyton Gray.'

'Lovely, if you just want to take a seat, Mrs Gray, I'll let Stella know that you've arrived.'

'Sorry.' I respond quickly. 'It's Miss. I'm not married.'

'Oh, I do apologise. I'll just get that amended on the system.'

Looking around I notice that I am the only person in the reception area, other than Maya of course and one other receptionist. It's kind of comforting to know that they don't have people lined up, one in one out, kerching goes the till.

'Miss Gray?' A tall, blonde, startling beautiful woman asks. Are they all beautiful here? Is that a prerequisite for working here?

'That's me.' I answer stupidly. It couldn't be anybody else.

'Smashing. Would you like to come through?'

I want to say no. No, I do not want to.

I want to go home. Forget this ridiculous idea of unburdening myself of these nightmarish memories, but I do not. I just nod my head and make my way into a cosy little lounge-type room in varying shades of coral.

Taking a seat I clutch my handbag to my chest and stare blindly at the lady named Stella. 'I'm sorry.' I begin, 'I don't know how this works, I don't know what I'm supposed to do.'

'Why don't we start at the beginning.' She takes a seat herself and opens up a notebook. 'What brings you here today?'

Shaking my head I know instantly that this will not work for me, because I cannot possibly answer that question.

What brings me here today?

Well, doc I'm living a nightmare, I think I'm being hunted by my crazed husband, who raped, beat and tormented me daily for the whole of our time together.

What brings me here?

The fear that I feel daily, my inability to sleep without waking in a panic, my illogical response to words that should just be words, my desperation to be loved but being unable to stop the paranoia that all men are out to get me and my hatred of colours together and tins in bloody order!

What brings me here today?
Well, I think I'm losing my mind.

'I can't do this.' I mumble as I make my way unsteadily towards the door, 'it was a mistake, I'm so sorry for wasting your time.'

'Miss Gray, why don't we just sit anyway, just for a few moments. I promise I won't ask you anything, we don't have to speak at all if you don't want to.'

'You must have other people that need your help.' I sigh as I twist the doorknob, 'you should help them. You can't help me.'

'Still.' She motions towards a big comfy-looking armchair in front of the bay window, 'we could just sit. What's the worst that could happen, just sitting.'

'It's just... I thought I could do this. But how can I talk to you, a total stranger, when I can't even speak to my parents about this, or Jake, or even myself sometimes.'

'Sometimes it's easier to tell a stranger our worries?' she suggests.

'I suppose.' I whisper, 'but I don't know where to start. Your first question was *what brings me here today*, I don't know. I just want to live I guess; I just want to stop being scared.'

'And what is it that you are afraid of?'

'My past. My husband. Not ever having my life back again.' I sigh, 'I'm not sure an hour is going to give us much time to cover the never-ending list of what scares me.'

'We don't have to cover everything in this first session. You've already taken a huge step by coming here today. Many people don't even make it through the front door. You should be proud of that achievement.'

'Does this work, honestly? All this talking?'

'It can do, yes. It's certainly a good place to start.'

'And do you think you can help *me*?'

Smiling, she steeples her fingers and rests them against her chin, 'I do, yes.'

'Then I guess I'm prepared to try. But it won't be easy listening, that I can assure you.'

'I know it's difficult.' She begins, once again opening up her notebook, 'suddenly being asked to discuss things that you've kept to yourself for so long, unearthing things that you've buried deep within yourself, but we do this at your pace. If you want to sit in silence for an hour, we can. If you want to rant and scream and cry, you can. This is on your terms.'

'I'm not so used to things being on *my terms*.'

'That's what I'm here for.' She smiles, 'to help you see that moving forward with your life, finding yourself again must always be on your own terms. I know you must think I'm just some woman sitting in a comfy chair who has no idea what you are going through, but I do.' She sighs, 'which is why I know that I can help you. It will take time and a lot of effort and emotional strain on your part, but it will be worth it.'

'I just don't know if I'm ready. I've hidden this part of me for so long, I don't know if bringing it all out into the open is wise.'

'Why don't we try? If not today, then at our next session? If not at that session, then the next? On your terms.'

Nodding, I glance out of the window at the street below, watching as people go about their lives, remembering the days that I would watch tourists and families from my balcony in Whitby, wishing I too could be just like them. I assumed that those people were carefree, that they had no worries, no torment, but I know now that I was wrong, because nobody has a clue what happens behind closed doors. Nobody!

It's been two weeks since I last saw Jake, and as I watch him now through my bedroom window, heading towards the fete, I know that I owe him an apology, as well as an explanation for my peculiar behaviour.

I have avoided him, I know that I have, and it's ridiculous. To lose two weeks of my life, hiding away like a recluse because of one silly little word, and my inability to fully open up to a professional, even though I'm sure now that she would be able to help me in time.

Jake tried to call me, and text, but by day four, when I hadn't responded to him, he had stopped. I could take the cowards way out now and text him instead of talking face to face, I could continue to avoid him, I could stay in bed and forget all about the fete – but I won't. I can't.

How can I ever move on with my life if I continue to be intimidated by a man who does not even know where I am? Eric could be busy living the high life for all I know, all memory of me wiped clean from his mind – while I stop living any kind of life. How can that possibly be fair? No. I will not allow him to rule me from afar anymore. Eric is my past, Jake could potentially be my future, and I will not let him take this away from me.

I will shower, make myself presentable and I will face this day as it should be faced – with happiness, confidence, and peace. I will try and drag the Jade of old back, kicking and screaming if I must – but I will not let anyone or anything ruin this day. We have all so worked hard to create this fete, this fun day, this extravaganza, and I will not miss out again because of Eric bloody Sawyer!

There is bunting everywhere!

Colourful triangles stretch high above our heads, so bright and cheerful as they sway gently in the light breeze – and I just know that Alf is somewhere pretending that he doesn't care for bunting, but secretly enjoying it, while Dorothy does her best to keep him away from *The Bingley Arms* for just one afternoon.

It won't be long before people start to arrive, and as I make my way across to my designated post on the raffle stand, I take in the rest of the stalls and attractions being prepared.

Around the back of the village hall is a beautiful bowling green, where a bowls competition will be held from 1PM for both children and adults, with various prizes to be won, as well as face painting, a bouncy castle, and a fortune teller that has been set up on the tennis court.

The fortune teller is, in fact, Clara, which surprised everybody when she volunteered, as she is normally incredibly shy, but she looks fantastic in her veils and floaty skirt, draped in plastic gold and dangly jewellery. Of course, she isn't in fact a genuine fortune teller, well, that we're away of anyway – but any monies raised from her mystical predictions will all be sent to charity – so it's all for a good cause.

Placed across the large car park out front of the village hall are many different stalls selling everything from bric a brac to hot dogs, cakes and buns, toys, tea and coffee, cheeses and soft drinks. We even, with thanks to a local chap, have an ice cream van, which is sure to be a huge hit as the day is warming up nicely.

Inside the village hall itself, we have a disco, and later in the day a dance competition, again for both adults and children. We have rather amusingly called our dance competition 'Strictly Come Bardsey' which I'm sure will go down well with dedicated *Strictly Come Dancing* fans. On a darker note, and even though I promised myself that I would not let Eric interfere with it, there is just one thing that I know with absolute certainty I must do. Today, guaranteed, there will be photographs a plenty being taken, and I must at all costs avoid being snapped. I know that the chances of Eric seeing images from a village fete in Bardsey of all places are slight, but still, I will not take that risk.

Spotting Dorothy over by the big white blossom tree in front of the village hall, clipboard in hand, I wave and make my way over to her. Jake has not reappeared, but the fete is large, with lots of jobs to be done before we are ready to open to the public, and I'm sure he's busy somewhere – not avoiding me as my brain is leaning towards thinking.

'Hello, Peyton dearie.' Dorothy smiles warmly at me, 'are you feeling any better?'

'I am, thank you, really glad not to have missed all of this, it looks amazing! Where do you want me?' I ask while looking around once more for Jake, 'is there anything that I can be helping with?'

'I don't want you tiring yourself out dearie, not when you've only just begun to feel better.'

'I'm fine honestly, put me to work.' I laugh, 'idle hands and all that.'

'You can help Jemima with the disco if you want – I do believe she's having some kind of dilemma with the music box.'

'Music box?'

'Oh, you know, the radio pod thingy.'

'The iPod?'

'iPods, peapods, who even knows the difference these days.'

Chuckling, I promise Dorothy that I will help Jemima with the *peapod* in time to have the disco up and running. Making my way inside I can't help but feel a small buzz of excitement. Today is definitely going to be a wonderful day.

Somehow, four hours have passed with helping Jemima and making sure that my stall is laid out properly, and before I know it, we are open for business. Visitors are happily milling about in the glorious sunshine, and children are excitedly running from stall to stall, begging their parents for treats and toys, before eventually discovering the large castle-shaped bouncy castle over in the corner. Thankfully none of the mums and dads has let their children have hotdogs or burgers before venturing onto the inflatable, which I am sure everybody concerned is happy about!

My raffle stall is moderately busy and it's nice to have my mind on something pleasant for once and just be able to enjoy the day, the sunshine, and the conversation.

I still haven't seen Jake, though I know he is in charge of the hot dog and burger stall today, which is way across the car park from my raffle stall, I suppose I shall need to eat at some point, and it would give me the perfect excuse to see him.

'I'll take four tickets please love.' A gruff voice sounds from behind me, 'four winners if you please.'

'Well, while I can't promise winners, I can promise that your money will be used wisely.' I smile, taking in the man before me. Does he look familiar? Am I just being paranoid?

'Do I know you?' he asks now, his voice uncertain as his eyes bore into mine.

'I don't believe so.' I whisper, suddenly overcome with paranoia.'

'No. No, I'm sure that I do. Give me a minute, it'll come to me.'

Handing the man his tickets I slowly turn away from him, trying desperately to steady my heart, just stay calm, breathe.

'I'm sure I know you.' He frowns, clearly puzzled, 'but where from?'

'I'm sure it'll come to you.' I murmur, trying to avoid eye contact. 'Maybe have a wander about, see if that helps.'

'Hmm, maybe.' Putting his tickets in his pocket he begins to walk away, only to stop again and glare at me, suspicious, determined to work me out. 'I've got it.' He declares loudly with a grin. 'I know *exactly* where I know you from.'

Readying myself to make my excuses and leave, I feel my heart begin to beat faster, my palms becoming sweaty – who is this man? Does he know Eric? Am I in danger?

Wiping damp palms against my dress, I slowly turn to face him. 'Oh?' I smile nervously.

'You are the absolute double of my son's Maths teacher. Mrs Robinson, Not related, are you?'

Relief floods through me. He does not know me.

'Nope, sorry.' I smile, 'but they do say everybody has a doppelganger don't they.'

'Yeah, I've heard that.' He smiles back, clearly impressed with himself for having worked out his mini mystery. 'Well, I'll leave you be then, what time is the raffle drawn?'

'A bit later, around four thirty I believe.'

'Great – here's hoping I have the winning tickets.'

Laughing, I wave the man off as he goes in search of food and decide that now would be a great time to take a break myself. It wasn't a close call, he doesn't know me, but still, my head is reeling, and the sun suddenly feels stifling hot on my face. I need a moment alone. A minute just to decompress.

A quick text message to Sally has my stalled covered, and as I head towards the village hall I catch a glimpse of Jake, just as he catches a glimpse of me.

'Peyton.' He calls out, as he rushes towards me holding two ice-cold bottles of pop, 'you look like you could do with one of these. Hot, isn't it?'

Jake looks as wonderful as always. So neat and tidy, not a hair out of place. What on earth he must think of me is anybody's guess, I always feel somewhat mismatched lately. Taking the cold drink, I sink onto the small wooden bench situated just outside of the village hall and smile at the giggles and screams of delight coming from within as children and adults bop around to *Girls Aloud*.

'Jake I…'

'You know if…'

We begin speaking at the same time and as our words collide, we chuckle, 'you first.' I prompt, taking another welcome sip of my drink.

'I was just going to say that if you aren't feeling up to being here, with the crowds and the noise… everybody would understand.'

'What? No.' I smile, 'I'm fine, honestly. I was actually just going to apologise for pretty much ghosting you these past two weeks. I feel so much better now, honestly. It was probably just some bug going around.'

'If you're sure.' He mumbles, 'it's just I was so worried about you, and you weren't answering your phone or messages. I didn't know what to do and then you show up this morning looking the picture of health and my head is just spinning. What's going on? Why were you avoiding me?'

'Jake, I was unwell, I wasn't avoiding you intentionally.' I respond angrily, 'I just needed time to rest up.'

'But you didn't respond to even one text Peyton, and I sent you enough.'

'Yeah, I know. Thirty-seven at last count.' Alarm bells ringing, I throw my bottle of pop in the bin and make my way back to my stall, I don't need this, I really don't. Not again.

'Wait up!' he calls after me, 'I wasn't having a go at you, I was just letting you know how I felt.'

'Yeah, I get it. Abandoned. Poor Jake!' I snap. 'Maybe we do need some time apart after all.' I suggest, 'Maybe you need to work on your abandonment issues.'

'Don't you think you're overeating just a little bit?' he asks with a frown, 'I hardly have abandonment issues.'

'Really? Because you're doing a really good impression of

somebody that does. Christ Jake, I can't even be unwell without getting the third degree!'

'Third degree? When have I ever done that?'

Realising instantly that I am projecting my past experiences onto Jake, I slow down trying to reassess the situation before me. Okay, so maybe it was just one outburst, one moment of frustration, and maybe I am being overly sensitive, but that's how it started before, exactly how it started before. Deciding that I need to be away from him, I ignore his question and carry on walking towards my stall.

'Peyton, c'mon, I'm sorry okay.' Grabbing my arm, he pulls me towards him and kisses my forehead. 'I'm sorry. Can we just forget the whole thing?'

Sighing I look up into his sad eyes and shake my head, 'I'm not going to spend my time arguing with you Jake, or explaining my whereabouts, do you understand that?'

'I do, I'm sorry. Can we just rewind all of my bullshit and start again?'

'I've got to get back.' I say, purposely avoiding his question, 'Sally will be wondering where I am.'

'Are we cool?' he hollers out as I walk away, 'Peyton?...'

I know that it's wrong of me to leave Jake wondering if we are okay, but his reaction to my temporary sickness really has pissed me off. I can understand his frustration and his concern for me, but it's not like he didn't know I was unwell, he helped me home for crying out loud.

I know that I'm not going to make him suffer forever, but a few more hours should definitely teach him a lesson.

As rain clouds begin to gather overhead, I look around at the now dwindling crowds, thankful that the day is nearly over. Raffle drawn, the man from earlier was pleased to discover that he did indeed have winning tickets and was more than happy with his fondue set – *an unwanted Christmas gift donated by Dorothy*. What we didn't tell anybody was that all of the tickets were in fact winners, as Dorothy doesn't like to see anybody disappointed. She may be tough on the outside, but she's soft and squishy on the inside, not that she'd ever admit that of course.

It has been a great day in terms of raising funds, however not so great in terms of arguing with Jake and memories of the past rearing their ugly heads.

I want to avoid Jake, not keen to revisit his apologies and my anger, so feigning tiredness, and feeling guilty for it, I leave Sally and Clara to clear away my stall and make my way home. All I need now is silence, a hot bath and a good book.

Wearily pushing open my front door I head towards the kitchen and dump my handbag onto the table, enjoying, as I do every time I come home, the peace and quiet.

Flicking the kettle on, I wait impatiently for it to boil as I kick off my sandals and dream of my hot bath. I don't currently have a book on the go, so making my way into the lounge I decide to re-read my favourite book, *Molly's Million* written by *Victoria Connelly.*

Grabbing the book, I freeze – something is wrong in here, slightly askew, but what? Looking around warily I begin to back out of the lounge slowly, someone has been here, I can feel it.   Nearly at the door now I finally realise what is wrong…

The blinds.

The blinds have been shut to the left!

Unable to move, I cannot help but stare at the blinds as my heart pounds erratically in my chest – is he here right now? Is he watching me?

Did I shut them that way?

Dropping my book, I race back into the kitchen and grab the largest of the kitchen knives from the magnetic strip above the cooker - is he still in the house?

I can't think, what the hell do I do? Call the police? Run away again? Hide?

Rummaging through my bag I slip my phone out and begin to dial 999. But what will I tell them? That I'm hiding from my abusive ex-husband, that Peyton isn't my real name, that he's moved the bloody blinds! They'll think I'm insane, not to mention what my friends and neighbours will think if a police car pulls up outside. My secret will come out, and I'll have to leave.

No.

He needs to know that he cannot do this to me. I have a new life now, a life that does not involve him. If he's here then I need to find him!

I know that my bravado is false, I know that if he suddenly appears before me, I will freeze, terrified of his anger, but what choice do I have?

'Eric?' I squeak, as I make my way towards the bottom of the stairs, absolutely petrified. 'Eric, are you here?'

Consciously avoiding the fourth step from the bottom, I smile despite my situation. When I first moved here, I was bothered by the creaky step, knowing for sure that it would eventually get on my nerves, until I realised one sleepless night that the step was in fact a blessing in disguise. Intruders could never know that that particular step groaned loudly the moment your foot trod upon it, and I felt happy with the realisation that it was in fact an early warning system of sorts. But now, this very step could be my undoing, drawing Eric's attention to where I am exactly in the house. The knife feels heavy in my hand as I make my way slowly to the top, my phone still prepped to dial 999. Cautiously pushing open the bathroom door, I recall the many times that I would watch movies just like this - long before Eric - yelling at the TV as I wonder why the hell she is walking so bloody slowly – rush him for crying out loud! Use the element of surprise! But I cannot, I am too afraid. Thankfully I have a shower screen in this house and not a shower curtain because if this were a movie, then you can guarantee that it would be closed and I'd have to suffer the trepidation of yanking it open. The bathroom is clear, there are no cupboards to check, and nothing has been moved around that I can see.

With shaky hands I close the bathroom door, avoiding my reflection in the mirror and make my way into the bedroom, knowing that I must check under the bed and in the wardrobes – both of which leave me vulnerable to a sudden attack – both leaving Eric the element of surprise. I should just leave now, run into the street, and seek assistance, that's what I'd be screaming at the telly! But with a deep breath, I drop quickly to my knees and scan beneath the bed - nothing. I fling open the wardrobe doors, and again, nothing! My clothes are still a mish-mash of colours, some half hanging off of their hangers – not orderly at all – he hasn't been in here.

Tins! The bloody tins! Rushing down the stairs and flinging open the kitchen cupboards I cry out as I take in the items before me, sinking to the floor as my whole body begins to shake. They are not ordered at all! They are a perfect mess of beans with spaghetti, custard with spam and soup with tinned fruit. He isn't here!

But what of the blinds?

Have I done that subconsciously?

Is it so ingrained in me that I have done it without thinking?

I must admit that I was in a bit of a rush this morning, my mind on a million things – but did I do that? Would I?

Knowing that I will not be able to relax in a bath now or get lost in my book, I make sure to shut the blinds to the right and taking my phone up to the bedroom I wedge the door shut with a chair. I will not sleep tonight. I will not sleep until I know for certain that I did shut those blinds to the left. Because I do not think that I did.

The night was long, minutes felt like hours, the house suddenly making noises that I am sure I have never heard before, with each creak and groan I felt certain that Eric was in the house, waiting to pounce, waiting for sleep to draw me in – I had dared not close my eyes or let the knife out of my sight – I had dared not move.

But today is another day – he did not come for me during the night and I can only assume now, in the light of day that I did indeed close the blinds to the left, I just hadn't realised what I was doing. I will pay closer attention in future; I will be more careful.

Forcing myself to my feet I glance warily in the mirror, grimacing at the sight before me. The dark circles beneath my eyes are only outdone by the wild look on my face and my flat lifeless hair. I am meeting the girls in just over an hour for coffee and to catch up on how well the fete had gone, but all I really want to do is sleep.

I cannot let them down; I know that I have been a flake lately and eventually it will come to a point where they just stop inviting me to things altogether and where will that leave me? Paranoid and friendless, that's where!

A shower will perk me right up I'm sure, thankful again that I don't have a shower curtain – re-runs of *Psycho* I do not need!

'**G**ood morning, Peyton' Hollers Sally across the café,

'feeling better?'

Our little café, 'Munchies' isn't the busiest in the world, but it's homely and welcoming, and as I glance across the room at the smiling faces before me, I am thankful to have made such wonderful friends. The warm feeling deep inside me, a complete contrast to the horror I used to face when I was permitted to leave the house, dreading being caught up by an old friend, dreading being late back. And so I soak it in, let it wash over me and through me, let myself just be happy in the moment.

Tucking my handbag beneath my chair, I smile at the ladies in turn and apologise for rushing away yesterday, 'I just came over all funny and tired.' I begin to explain, 'I'm so sorry that I left you to tidy away my stall, I felt terrible about it.'

'Well…' Jemima our resident busy body frowns, 'I'm sure that the little tiff that you had with Jake didn't exactly help matters, everything okay on that front? It looked somewhat heated?'

'Oh shush those lips of yours.' Snaps Dorothy, 'at least she has somebody to *tiff* with!'

'That's hardly called for.' Jemima responds with a huff, 'I was merely asking if the girl was okay.'

'Nothing you do is *merely asking* it's just another line in your gossip book! Don't think I don't know that you're writing a book about us all.'

'Well, I never…'

'Yes, you should try that, never being so nosey.'

'A book?' I squeak, nervously, 'I'm not in it am I?'

'There isn't a book.' Sulks Jemima, 'it's just a collection of… memories.'

'I think I'd quite like to be in a book.' Sally pipes up, 'so long as I get a juicy part.'

'You *are* the juicy part.' Laughs Dorothy.

'And what exactly is that supposed to mean?'

'Ladies, ladies.' I chuckle, 'why don't we order our coffees and…'

'No, no, I want to know what's in this book that makes me the *juicy part*.' Demands Sally, 'well…' she stares at Jemima, 'what is it?'

'It's nothing. There are no juicy parts.'

'Oh, too boring are we?' Dorothy winks, 'well I'll have you know…'

'We don't want to know.' Snaps Jemima, 'you just keep your shenanigans with Alf to yourself!'

'Coffee?' I ask, desperate not to be dragged into this argument. Christ, can you just imagine if there was indeed a book?

'My shenanigans with that husband of mine would give you at least seven good chapters!'

'It isn't *Fifty Shades* you know!'

'Ha! So there is a book, I knew it!'

'I'll get the coffee.' I say to nobody in particular, leaving the girls arguing about a book that will probably never see the light of day.

At the counter, I order five Lattes and as the coffee machine burbles and bubbles, I step outside and take in the beauty before me. It's so peaceful and green in Bardsey, the air smells clean and fresh, and the only noise, other than the ladies inside arguing now about whether there are photos in this mystery book, is bird song. I have most certainly landed on my feet here in Bardsey.

Glancing across towards the Village Hall, I swear I see movement, a shadow. Squinting and acknowledging that I should book an eye test, I try to bring the distance into focus. There is definitely a man lurking at the side of the Village Hall and he's looking right at me.

Unsure if I should wave, I just stand frozen, like a deer caught in the headlights, who the hell is it?

Naturally, my first thought after last night's episode is Eric, but I am sure, as I was so monumentally wrong last night that it's either Alf or somebody just passing through, who, like myself, is just taking a moment to enjoy the peace. But why then does he not move?

If I were braver, if I weren't a scared little mouse these days, I would amble over, introduce myself, and ask what he's doing, but I know that I will never do that.

'What's taking so long with these blasted coffees?' Dorothy's voice booms from behind me, making me jump just a little. 'What are you gaping at out there?'

'There's a man…' I begin, pointing across to where he stands, still, so perfectly still.

'Well what the heck is he doing just standing there?' she asks, bemused, 'I shall ask him.'

'Dorothy, I don't think…'

But she's gone, marching across the road, a woman on a mission. 'Good morning.' She hollers, 'lovely day for a stroll, isn't it?'

The man does not respond, he does not wave, he does not move, he just continues to stare right at me.

'*I said* good morning.' Dorothy begins again, this time a little annoyed at being ignored. But as she draws nearer to the man, he suddenly turns and walks away. No acknowledgement of Dorothy's presence or greeting, no nothing, he just vanishes. 'Well, I never! How rude! Blooming tourists!' With a grunt at his retreating back,

Dorothy throws her hands up in the air and shakes her head. 'Let's get those coffees shall we dear.'

Smiling, I follow Dorothy back inside, convinced now that the stranger is not a plain ol' tourist at all.

It's been a pleasant afternoon with the ladies after I pushed the mystery man to the back of my mind, even shy Clara had a few choice words to say about this book of Jemima's, which shocked us all. I had had a moment of peculiar reflection as I had sat sipping my Latte while half listening to the comments being flung back and forth across the table – these were my new friends. These elderly dears that held nothing back had somehow welcomed me in, almost like a temporary replacement to my old friends, my old circle. A circle that I wished to see very much restored. Of course, I know that this friendship can never replace the years of loyalty and trust that I have with Heidi, Nicky, Jess, and Gordon, but for now, I welcome it. I need it.

Feeling relaxed, at last, I decided to text Jake and ask him if he fancied a night out, nothing too heavy, just a few drinks at the local, but as the afternoon ended and he had still not responded I could only draw on the conclusion that he was still upset over out argument, and it was, in fact, him avoiding me and not the other way around as I had envisaged.

I did wonder, despite trying my hardest not to, that if the stranger was indeed Eric would he by now be aware of my on/off relationship with Jake?

And just what would he do if he was?

Sliding the key into the lock of my cottage, I pause as the fears of last night begin to slowly creep their way back into my mind. Could it really have been him standing there, watching me? I cannot for the life of me work out how he would have done that. Gordon and I made sure that every trace of my move here was covered – I have no social media, no bank cards, no mortgage, or name on a tenancy – I am a ghost. So how could it have been him?

But still, the way that the shadow man just stood there, staring, unflinching, blatant, has me double-checking once more that the house is clear, that he does not lurk in some hidden place ready to pounce.

If it had been him, I wonder what he made of me now? My lovely hair has grown long again, my made-up face smiling as I laugh with my new friends, my clothes no longer frumpy and unattractive, my new life without him. If it had been him then I know only too well the anger that would have been bubbling up deep inside his veins, ready to burst, ready to unleash a torrent of hell upon me.

If it had been him then I know exactly what is heading my way.

Shrugging off the darkest of thoughts, I make my way as calmly as I can up the stairs. I will check each room methodically, I will leave no cupboard door unopened, and no under-bed space left unchecked. I will not let him surprise me. If he is here, then despite my fear, despite the tremors that cause my hands to shake involuntarily, I will face him. I will face him and tell him to leave.

I will not. I know I will not.

I am not that brave.

The wardrobes are clear, other than the disarray and rainbow of clothes shoved together haphazardly on hangers, in no order whatsoever. The bathroom is empty, behind every door is checked, as well as under every bed. The tins remain a mixture of foods and the blinds are still shut the way that I left them. He is not here.

Maybe he never was.

I'm just being paranoid. Ghosts of the past are popping by to snatch away the happiness that I have made for myself, well, they can just piss right off – this is my happiness and they are not having it!

Slipping into my pyjamas I decide that a night in front of the TV with a big glass of wine is most certainly in order. My nerves have been shot these past few days.

Skipping past the horror and romance sections on Netflix, I certainly do not need either of those! I head straight for comedy and settle upon something cheesy that I won't need to pay too much attention to.

I still haven't heard from Jake, so I guess that is that then. Our relationship or whatever the hell it was ended before it even really began. He could at least have had the decency to tell me.

I do appreciate the double standards, after-all I have all but ghosted Jake for a fortnight, which must have been difficult for him to understand. Maybe I should just be brave, tell him what happened to me, tell him my secrets, at least then he would know what he was getting himself into.

If he responds, and I hope that he does, I will take off this mask that I wear, I will shed Peyton Gray, just for him and I will lay myself bare.

I may not have been able to tell the therapist about my demons in that first session, but for Jake, I will be brave.

Nodding off I am startled awake suddenly by the

telephone ringing. With bleary eyes I note that the film I had been watching is long finished and the time is 21.45pm, I must have done more than nod I muse as I reach out to grab my phone from the table beside the settee.

'Hello?' I yawn into the handset, hoping beyond hope that it's not some stupid telemarketing call.

'Jade, it's me, Heidi, did I wake you?'

Heidi and Gordon are the only people that I trust enough to have my new pay-as-you-go telephone number. It's not that I don't trust Nicky and Jess, but they are a little forgetful and carefree with their gadgets and I could not risk either of their phones falling into Eric's hands. Not can I trust my mum and dad – purely because they would store the number as *Jade's new secret number*!

'No, no, I'm awake.' I yawn again, 'I mean I was asleep, yes, but I'm awake now.'

'Look I can call you back if you want, but I have something you might want to know.'

Intrigued I prompt her to spill the beans, which she does, in true Heidi fashion, without taking a breath.

'So, you remember Eric the dicksplash telling you and your folks that his parents are dead as dodos, right? Well, that was a big fat lie! They are both very much alive, very well and very bloody nice!'

'Wait, what? How do you know this?'

'Ha glad you asked.' She chuckles, 'they both have *Facebook*! Can you believe that! No wonder he didn't want you to have any social media. Anyway, I contacted them on there, sent them some cryptic little message about it being super important I spoke to them about their son, and guess what…?'

'What?' I ask, knowing that I needn't add more.

'They sent one right back, saying that they'd speak to me but only if I could guarantee that Eric the knobjockey wouldn't find out – my words, not theirs. So I go right ahead and arrange a little clandestine meeting with them at some seriously shady hotel …'

'What? Heidi for gods…'

'I'm joking, I'm joking, they invited me to their house for tea – let me tell you it is well posh! They didn't beat around the bush either with dishing the dirt on Eric the…'

'Okay, okay I get the picture.' I laugh, 'Eric the cockwomble right?'

'Jade Locke, you shock me, cockwomble indeed.' She hollers down the phone. 'They only go and tell me right off the bat that he was a terrible child, always bullying some poor kid, and then later his girlfriends! He was by all accounts a devious little shit, always lying and scheming, always blaming somebody else for his actions. His own dad expressed concerns that his son was a psychopath and would probably end up killing somebody.

I told them all about you Jade, what he'd done and they were not surprised! They were upset for you, but not surprised by him! His own parents! Obviously, I had to tell them that he was telling anyone that would listen that they were pushing up daisies - again, not surprised!'

'Did they say why? Why they're not surprised that he tells people they're dead?' I think back to that day at my parents' home, he was so convincing, and I felt so horrid for him, I pitied that small boy that grew up with no mum and dad.

... *'it was a boating accident. I was just a kid, so I don't remember too much myself. I think my father had a little too much liquid confidence in himself, and not nearly enough knowledge of boats. He crashed the boat, mum and dad drowned, I somehow didn't. I can't really remember much about it.'*...

'Oh yeah! They had some big ding-dong, a few years before he met you. He was engaged to some lovely little thing called Amber, a model wannabe, with a face that could launch a thousand ships kinda thing – and all was well until one night he came home drunk and found her and her best friend Carly packing her bags, she was done with his shit! Well, you know only too well how that situation goes down with a fucker like him – there was a fight, and poor Amber is screaming like a bloody banshee and the neighbours call the cops – by the time they arrive he's buggered off, the best friend who was helping Amber pack at the time was hiding in the bathroom absolutely petrified – and Amber? Well, let's just say her beautiful face couldn't even launch a Dinghy! He beat her so badly that's she permanently disfigured now!'

My heart is beating ten to a dozen as I imagine the fear that those two innocent women must have felt. A fear that I know only too well. 'And him?' I ask, 'Surely the police found him? Surely, he was arrested and charged?'

'You'd think so, right? Nope! Neither of the women pressed charges, they made it perfectly clear that if he was arrested, they would vanish, they would never speak out against him.'

'How does he get away with this?' I cry, 'How does one man flit through life leaving carnage wherever he goes and is never held accountable!'

'Because he might be a monster Jade, and he is, but he's a charming monster – that's how.'

'So how do his parents know all of this, about Amber, if they wouldn't talk about it?'

'Because they helped Amber start a new life, far far away from their shitty son. Turns out that even after the attack he would not leave her alone, he was obsessed with her. So she turned to them, begged them to help her, and they did. Eric found out and that was the massive ding dong – he felt they had betrayed him and they told him that he was no longer their son, they haven't seen him since and they have sworn me to absolute secrecy that he never finds out where they live now. They never want him back in their lives ever again!'

'Jesus!' I sob, as tears fall down my face, 'that could have been me, Heidi, if I hadn't escaped that could have been me.'

'Jade honey, it already is you.'

As we both fall silent, I can hear Heidi sniffling down the phone line, the drama of the story finally sinking in. He may not have disfigured my face, but he has damaged me. Damaged me irreparably.

'There's one more thing.' Heidi begins, 'he came to see me a few weeks ago, at work of all places. Demanding that I tell him where you are, it was awful, everyone was staring.

So I lied Jade, I told him that we aren't friends anymore, that your disappearing act was a massive betrayal of our friendship and that I never wanted to see or hear from you again. I don't know if he believed me, but he left not long after. It broke me to say those words about you, but you know that they're not true, you know that I love you like a sister. You do know that, right?'

'Of course I know that.' I smile, 'You *are* my sister and one day when this nightmare is finally over, we can be a family again, I promise you we will be.'

'I wasn't going to tell you, but…'

'No, I'm glad that you did.'

'Any more thoughts on going to the police?'

Heidi knows it's not a question I like, she knows that I'm not mentally prepared to deal with the fallout from that, but I can understand too why she feels the need to ask.

'One day.' I sigh, 'But not today.'

It's the same answer that I always give her, the same answer that she always expects, and I do hope that one day I can surprise her with a different response, but right now I cannot.

'I have seen a therapist.' I offer up, 'Well, it was an initial appointment, and I didn't really say much, but…'

'Honey that's fantastic! I am proud of you you know.'

'I know.' I smile down the phone, 'I just hope one day all of this will seem like some horrid nightmare.'

'It will. I don't know how long it will take, but one day you will come home Jade, and we will all be waiting for you.'

We talk a little longer, each wishing that we were face to face, that we could have these chats in person until the clock chimes midnight and we both realise that we have been chatting for just over two hours – some things never change.

Wishing her goodnight, I grab a glass of water from the kitchen and begin making my way up to bed when the phone rings again. Laughing I pick up the phone, 'Okay, what goss haven't you told me?'

There is only silence.

'Heidi? Have you butt-dialled me? Heidi? Seriously, you are useless with technology. I'm hanging up, okay?'

A slight crackling begins, like the start of a song being played on vinyl...

...By the light of the silvery moon
I want to spoon
To my honey, I'll croon love's tune
Honey moon, keep a-shinin' in June
Your silvery beams will bring love's dreams

We'll be cuddlin' soon
By the silvery moon...

PART FOUR

THE PAST RETURNS...

Barricaded in the ensuite bathroom, I had watched the hours pass slowly from midnight to now, 08.37 AM.

I had not run out into the night in a blind panic, despite my entire being screaming at me to do so. I had forced myself to remain calm, dragged the chest of drawers from the bedroom into the bathroom and rammed them against the door. I had seen the long night through, terrified and alone with the largest of the kitchen knives clutched protectively against my chest. I could not flee into the darkness, even though I desperately wanted to. Because I knew in my panic I would not see him, but he would most certainly see me.

He knows that he has me running scared now. He knows that I will try once more to escape him.

I can't stay here, it's no longer safe. I'll pack lightly and call Gordon and Heidi once I'm on the bus. Anything that I leave behind, Gordon, I'm sure, will pack up for me. How the hell did he find me, I've been so careful. I've done everything right. But I knew. I knew he would never stop looking for me.

Throwing clothes and toiletries haphazardly into my beloved suitcase, I rush down the stairs, desperate to flee this house, the only place that has ever truly been a sanctuary to me since Eric bulldozed his way into my life. Hand on the door handle I am frozen as the telephone begins to ring, is it him again?

I could just ignore it, pretend that I haven't heard its incessant trilling, but what if it's Heidi, what if there is an emergency?

What if it's him?

He can't hurt me through a receiver I rationalise, and as I press the green answer button with shaking hands I whisper a nervous hello.

'Hello? Am I speaking with Miss Peyton Gray?' The voice is friendly, female, and not at all threatening. But still, I can't be too careful.

'May I ask who's calling?' I respond, neither confirming nor denying my identity.

'This is Nurse Woodhouse, I have you down as the next of kin for Mr Jake Walker. Is this Miss Peyton Gray?'

'Next of kin?' I splutter, 'What has happened? Is Jake okay?'

'You are Miss Peyton Gray then I take it?'

'I am yes, please, please just tell me what's happened.'

I know it's him. I know Eric has done something dreadful. Next of Kin? Does that mean he's...

'I'm sorry to have to inform you that Mr Walker has been involved in an attack. He's...'

'Dead?' I whisper, 'is he dead?'

'No, no of course not, he's just pretty bashed up, it seems like he took one hell of a beating though. He asked if we could call you, just to let you know what was happening.'

'But he's okay?'

'He'll live. Nothing that bed rest and a little TLC won't solve.'

'Can I come in? To see him?'

'Absolutely. We do want to keep him in, just for observation, check for signs of concussion, that kind of thing, but other than that, yes, he can receive visitors.'

'Thank you.' I sigh, 'Thank you for letting me know. I'll just arrange some transport and I'll be with you shortly.'

Hanging up on the nurse, I quickly dial for a taxi. Before I leave Bardsey for good, I must ensure that Jake is well and that there is no permanent damage. Then I'll jump on the first bus I see and head in whichever direction it decides to take me.

I feel dreadful that I won't be saying goodbye to my friends, but the more people that know I'm leaving the easier it will be for Eric to pick up my trail. At least this way they can truthfully say they don't know where I am, or even, that they knew I was leaving, which will hopefully stall Eric enough to give me a head start.

Rushing through the hospital I quickly locate Jake's room and just take a moment while he remains oblivious to my presence to truly see the damage that Eric has caused.

Nurse Woodhouse was right, he has taken a hell of a beating. His poor face is swollen and bruised, he has a cut under one eye and a busted lip, as well as his arm in a sling.

I'm right to leave, even if it just means that no one else will suffer at the hands of my husband.

'Peyton?' Jake's voice breaks through my musings, 'I'm so glad that you came.'

Throwing my arms around him I apologise over and over for what has happened to him, only stopping as he winces in pain at my overly enthusiastic hug.

'It's hardly your fault that some maniac jumped me. These are just the times we live in, though I'd never have expected it in Bardsey.'

'Did you see him? The attacker, I mean?'

'No. He just came from behind me. He didn't say one word to me either which I thought was odd, he also didn't mug me, so I don't know what the point of it all was.'

'He said nothing? Not one word?'

'Nope. Bizarre isn't it?'

'And what have the doctors said?' I ask, sadly, 'The nurse

that called me said they want to keep in? Is your arm broken?'

'They do, but what's the point? Somebody else, in a worse condition than I am, will probably need the bed. I think I'm going to discharge myself. The sling is just for sympathy.' He grins, 'Is it working?'

'Should you really leave?' I question, not wanting further harm to come to him. 'What if you have a concussion?'

'I won't sleep.' He winks, 'You can keep an eye on me.'

'The thing is, Jake.' I begin, unsure of what exactly I should tell him. He deserves to know who did this to him, he deserves to know because I brought this to him and because he should know who his attacker was. 'I need to leave, I can't explain why right now, but it's imperative that I do. For my safety, for yours, I must go.'

As I turn towards the door, Jake grabs my arm and asks what the hell is going on. Stifling a sob I fall against his chest and tell him that I need to leave Bardsey, for good.

'I don't understand? Peyton, look at me. Help me understand, please.' He begs, 'Is it something that I've done? Is it something to do with my attack? Do you know who did this to me?'

'I want to tell you, honestly, I do. But now isn't the time. I don't *have* time.'

'Is it the man that attacked me? Is he why you're so afraid? I mean, it would explain a lot.'

'What do you mean?' I ask, a little angry now. 'What would it explain?'

'I dunno.' He shrugs, 'You can be a little strange sometimes, hiding, all these mysterious illnesses.'

'One illness Jake! One! And I explained about that. Christ!' I fume, running a shaking hand through my tangled hair, 'I don't have time for this!'

'Okay, okay, I'm sorry. Let's not fall out. Let's just get me out of here and then we can talk.'

'I can't...'

'Look, whatever it is, or whoever it is, we can deal with it together. Just don't run out on me.'

'I just need to go, please Jake.'

'But, forever? I don't understand.'

How can I expect him to understand when I haven't told him one ounce of truth since we met.

'Look.' He smiles, tipping my face up to meet his, 'Let me get myself checked out of this place, then we can go away together. My parents have a summer house, we can hide away there, just me and you. What do you say? And then, if you feel able to, you can tell me what is going on?'

The thought of not rushing out into the world aimlessly

is appealing, and even Eric couldn't know where Jake's parents' summer house is. Nodding, I wipe away the tears that have fallen down my face and tell him that I will wait while he is discharged.

'No point, it could take a few hours for them to get around to sorting out the paperwork. I'll meet you at the café, okay, just please, promise me you won't take off?'

'Let's just go now.' I plead, 'Forget the paperwork.'

Kissing my forehead he smiles, 'I can't do that Peyton, that wouldn't be orderly.'

'Screw orderly Jake! I am sick and bloody tired of orderly!'

'I'll meet you at the café, okay? I just need to finalise things here, grab some things from home and then we can get going.'

'I can grab your things, I'll just need your keys.'

I want to be mistaken, I want to believe that the shadow that just flashed across his face is all in my imagination, but is it? It's a look I've seen many times over the years, am I ever likely to mistake it?

'That's really not necessary, I'll just meet you at the café once I've sorted everything out here.'

'Why can't I have your keys, Jake?'

Sighing, he pushes me gently towards the door, 'I'll meet

215

you at the café in a few hours, just don't leave without me.'

Confused I begin my long walk out of the hospital, careful not to stray away from the coloured lines on the floor.

Why couldn't I just have his keys?

What is he hiding?

Am I right to trust him?

Using the app on my mobile phone I request a taxi to pick me up at the front of the hospital, and as I debate whether or not to text Jake and tell him that I can't meet him, that it's better if I just go, I realise with horror that that is not an immediate option. In my rush to see him, I left my suitcase at home in the hallway.

I have no choice now but to go back.

Tentatively slipping the key into the lock I whisper a silent prayer that the door doesn't creak as it normally does.

I'm sure that he won't be here, lurking in the shadows, after all, he's had plenty of opportunities to pounce on me while I slept. When I've been at my most vulnerable.

But then, Eric doesn't work that way, does he?

No.

That's not traumatising enough for him. He likes the chase, he likes the knowledge that he makes me afraid. The terror of waking from sleep to find him at the end of my bed wouldn't last long enough for him – he likes to draw things out.

I am going to speak with the police I decide as I stand staring at the inoffensive front door. I can't continue like this. Scared to open a door! Not to mention what he has done to poor Jake. Enough is enough, I need to put an end to his sick games once and for all.

I won't let him have this power over me. If I speak with them, then I'm certain that I can finally put an end to this madness. They will keep him away from me.

The door *does* creak as I edge it open and so I decide I may as well just go with it, if he is here then he will already be aware of my presence. There is nothing more that I can do to enter this property quietly.

Grabbing my suitcase I am heading back towards the front door when I decide that I would like to take a book with me. Waiting for Jake could take a while. I dare not risk running up to the bedroom to grab my favourite book, I'm not brave enough, but there are plenty of other good ones on the bookcase, and it will just take a moment to select one. Just a moment.

Taking one last look at the front door, knowing that I could just walk out right now, and forget the book, forget my life here, forget my friends, forget Jake, I take a deep breath, push open the door to the living room and sprint inside.

Everything is exactly as I left it.

The blinds are fully shut, the pillows are a mess, and my bookcase is disorganised and chaotic. Everything is messy, just how I like it.

Reaching out I take the first book that is closest to me, *The house in the clouds*, another wonderful book by *Victoria Connelly*. I think the only way I'll ever have any peace is if I live in the clouds!

I'm now just a few steps away from my initial goal, but as I take one last look at the room that has sheltered me I know that I will not be completing that goal, as the living room door slowly closes behind me.

Paralysed, I try to steady my breathing and calm the panic rising within me. I know he's behind me, I can feel him, I can hear his breath, sense his anger, and yet, I cannot move. I want to run, but my body is frozen, and my legs are leaden. I'm like a rabbit trapped in headlights and the impact will, I know, most certainly be fatal.

Eric doesn't speak, but as he moves to stand behind me, his body pressed against mine, I can feel his hot breath on the back of my neck and his hands gripping my shoulders painfully.

Mouth dry, I bite back the scream that is building deep within me, I must not anger him further, I know the drill.

'Tut, tut, tut, *wife*.' He whispers in my ear, 'Running out on me again I see.'

'Eric, I…'

'Did you honestly think I'd let you go a second time?' he snarls, 'did you honestly think you could outsmart me?'

I want to scream that he never *let* me go, I escaped. I *did* outsmart him and it wasn't even hard to do! But the venom in his voice, the hatred, the hostility is overwhelming, he does genuinely hate me.

Pulling my arms behind my back he begins to push me from the room, and I feel all at once my desire to live kick in, increasing my heart rate, and flooding my entire body with adrenaline, I cannot go where he plans for me to go. If I do then I'm as good as dead.

'We have a lot of catching up to do wife. I think we'll start in the bedroom.'

Using as much body strength as I can muster I throw myself sideways against the wall, causing Eric to lose his grip and topple backwards. Throwing my book, I run for the front door, knowing it won't be long until he's behind me.

Rushing past my suitcase, I fling open the front door and run out into the garden, not stopping to look behind me, I race up the garden path, knowing that if I can get out onto the street I'll be safer.

'JADE!' Eric's voice bellows furiously behind me, as his footsteps pound up the garden path. 'Get back here!'

Reaching the gate now, I flick the latch and am almost through it when the full force of Eric's body slams into mine, sending me sprawling against the wall and bushes to the left of the gate. Scrambling, I try to get to my feet as brambles pull at my hair and scratch my face. Screaming now, I begin to thrash out as Eric looms over me, my legs kicking at his legs, anything to stop him from getting any closer.

'What did I just say about you trying to outsmart me, Jade? You're really not that smart! And stop that god-awful screaming!'

As he strikes my face with the back of his hand, my head snaps back against the sharp thorns of the rose bush behind me. Ignoring my howls of pain, he grabs my hair and begins to drag me back down the garden path, my legs unable to find purchase on the loose gravel.

'Let me go!' I wail as I try to reach up to where his large hands are pulling at my hair, 'I'll walk, please, just let me go.' My scalp burns as my hair is yanked from its roots, but I can't release his grip on me, and as he drags me through the front door and up the stairs I feel dizziness begin to blur my vision.

'**W**akey, Wakey Jadey.'

Blinking, I wince at the pounding behind my eyes, to find that I'm laying flat on the bed with Eric standing over me with a look on his face that immediately induces terror deep within me.

'I think we need to have a little chat, Jade.' He begins, 'Or is it Peyton now? I just cannot keep up with you. Nice place, by the way, courtesy of Gordon I presume?'

'Does it matter?' I whisper as I ease myself painfully up onto my elbows, 'I'd have lived on the streets to get away from you.'

'Now, now Jade, I can't understand why you would think that would be a better alternative to your life with me. Was I not good to you? Did I not provide you with everything that you needed? You sound a little ungrateful Jade.'

'Ungrateful?' I spit, 'You abused me, Eric! Every day of

our marriage I wanted to kill myself just to get away from you!'

'And yet you stayed.' He grins, 'So maybe you enjoyed it.'

'Enjoyed it? Enjoyed being raped, beaten, humiliated? What kind of lunatic would enjoy that?'

'You, clearly.'

'I left you, Eric, I *did* outsmart you – I left you because I hate you!'

'And yet you seem to like John? Or is it James? Did you let him fuck you, Jade? Did he fuck my wife?'

'His name is Jake. Didn't you ask him that before you beat him to a pulp?'

'I barely touched him.' He shrugs, 'Not much of a fighter this James of yours.'

'His name is *Jake*, and I've seen what you *barely touching* him looks like, you're a monster!'

'Did you let him fuck you, Jade?'

'What if I did.' I laugh, bitterly, 'He's ten times the man you are and it was *good*! It was *really good*!'

I know instantly that I have gone too far, and as he begins to unbuckle his belt I bolt for the door, only to be dragged back again and dumped onto the bed.

'I'll show you just what kind of man I am.' He growls in my ear as he yanks my jeans and knickers down around my ankles. Ten times better eh? Well, I'm sure I can exceed that.'

'No!' I scream, as he flips me onto my front and thrusts into me, hard and painful. 'No.' I sob, 'no.'

'Stop talking.' He grunts, pushing my face into the pillow, 'Just stop talking.'

'I hate you.' I Whimper, 'I hate you.'

'I said, stop fucking talking!' The punch to the back of my head instantly transports me back to our wedding night, and I close my eyes, praying that it ends soon, just as I had back then.

With a groan, he finishes and rolls himself to the opposite side of the bed. I'm sore, no doubt bleeding and I know that I am going to die in this room. Jake won't come looking for me, he'll just assume that I left without him. Once again I am alone in this hell, and I don't think I can get out of it this time.

'Shower. Now!' he commands as I curl myself up into the smallest ball that I can, 'You know I hate dirty women.'

'Really?' I sniff, 'because you sure had a lot of them when we were married.'

Slapping my hip, he rolls onto his side to face me, 'Just get in the shower Jade, unless of course, you want *me* to wash you?'

Not needing to be told again, I rush from the bed and into the bathroom, as Eric's laughter booms behind me.

'Oh, you won't find anything sharp in there Jade.' He chuckles, menacingly, 'I had a clear out while you were busy visiting lover boy!'

Ignoring him, I switch on the shower, not caring that it's still cold, I just need to wash him off of me and remove his mark.

Rubbing frantically I scrub until my skin is red, until I can no longer feel him inside me, until I can no longer smell him on my body. I know that it's a pointless exercise, this won't be the last time that he rapes me, I know how he works, and I know that hurting me makes him feel powerful. 'What's taking so long Jade? Do you need me to come in and help?

Switching off the shower, I hurriedly dry myself and pull my clothes back on in record time. Help from Eric I do not need.

'Shame.' He grins, as I walk back into the bedroom, wincing with each step that I take. 'I could have gone for round two.'

'What are we doing here, Eric? What exactly do you want from me?' I ask bravely. There isn't much more that he can do to me, everything terrible I could suffer at his hands I already have, a million times over.

'I would have thought that was obvious, wife.' He shrugs, as he pulls on his jeans, 'I've come to take you home. Where you belong.'

Sighing, I sit on the very edge of the bed, 'why? You don't love me, you don't even like me, so what's the point in our continuing this farce of a marriage?'

'Farce? Is that what you think our wedding vows were Jade? Because I meant them, every word.'

'Really?' I scoff, 'because you didn't stick to your vows when I was sick, you don't love me, and the only person honouring and obeying is me! So yeah, it's a farce.'

'But I never abandoned you, Jade. Not even when you tested me to my limits. I always came back to you.'

'*I* tested *you*? You tormented me daily! I'd have preferred it if you had stayed with one of your many other women!'

'This is getting us nowhere. You ran out on me, on our marriage, you broke your vows.'

'Our vows did not say that I would be abused, so yeah, I did run out on you because there wasn't an *us*, there never has been, there's only ever been *you*.'

'Three years Jade! For three years I've searched for you. Did you think that I'd just let you go?'

'I wish you had.'

'So you could carry on with James?'

'His name is *Jake!*'

'Whatever his name is, you can forget all about him. I have you back now and that is that unless, of course, you want me to pay him another little visit?'

'I'm not going back to Whitby with you.' I declare, sounding braver than I feel, 'I do not love you, I do not want to be with you, I hate you!'

'That doesn't matter, you'll soon fall back into your old routine.'

'I'll just run away again, and this time I'll double my efforts so that you will never find me.'

'Ah, but I've learnt so many ways to track down a missing person. Three years gives you an awful lot of time to hone your skills. I had a few non-starts when I initially began looking for you. Social media I quickly realised was not an option, your parents and those dumb friends of yours were a waste of space. So, I checked out your favourite places, childhood haunts, and things you'd told me from your past, but nada! You were gone. I did also think that you'd come back with your tail between your legs, but you surprised me again, you stayed away.'

'So how did you find me, Sherlock?'

Sliding closer to me on the bed, he puts his arm around

my shoulders and crushes me against him, 'ANPR! Well, you couldn't write it really.' He laughs, 'I bumped into an old schoolmate of mine – he's a cop now, and as you know, money talks. I slipped him a few hundred quid and he searched for the number plates of all your friends and family, and do you know whose pinged the loudest?' He doesn't expect me to guess, so I remain silent, 'Gordon! This mate of mine tracked you all the way to sweet little Bardsey.'

'How long have you known where I was?'

'Oh, not long, but enough to see how much you've changed, and it's not for the better.'

'Why not make your move sooner?'

'Because I enjoyed watching you.'

'So why now? Jealous of my relationship with Jake were you?'

'There is no relationship.' He snarls, and I know once again that I am in dangerous territory.

I'm afraid.

I'm afraid that I can't be silent anymore. I doubt I'm going to make it out of this room alive anyway, so if I push his buttons, if I make him mad, then so be it.

'Jake treats me well, and if you cared for me even one iota then you would let me go, you would let me be happy.'

'You will be happy. With me.'

'But I won't Eric, can't you see that? You don't love me, I'm just a possession to you. If you loved me then you wouldn't treat me so badly.'

'I'm only hard on you because I want you to be strong Jade. I want you to be everything that my mother wasn't.' Taking a deep breath, I stand slowly and make my way towards the window. 'I know that your parents aren't dead Eric. I know that they are very much alive and well. You are a liar! You are a bully and you are a rapist! This isn't about strength, or your mother, or helping me! It's about power and control and…'

'They're dead to me Jade.' He interrupts, 'Never mention them again.'

'And Amber?' I murmur, 'What about her?'

'What did you just say?'

He's calm as he moves to stand beside me at the window, it's a stillness that I know all too well. Eric, teetering on the edge, one wrong word, one wrong move could tip him over, hurtling him headfirst into a fiery unstoppable rage. I can't backtrack now, I've started and to go back on what I need to say would only cause me to suffer more.

'Amber.' I say, once more, chin up, defiant, 'I said what about Amber?'

He doesn't move, and he doesn't make a sound, but I can feel the tension building, I can feel the air around me crackle with animosity.

I do not expect the blow to my face, though by now I suppose that I should. Falling backwards I hit my back against the dressing table that sits to the right of the window, momentarily winding myself.

'Say her name again.' Eric roars, his face now just inches away from mine. 'Say it.'

I know that I shouldn't. I know that it's not a dare that I should respond to, but, I'm as good as dead anyway so why drag it out any longer.

'AMBER!' I scream into his face, 'AMBER, AMBER, AMBER!'

Grabbing handfuls of my hair he drags me into the bathroom and pulls open my bathroom cabinet, revealing all of the sharp objects that he told me had removed. Smiling to myself I chuckle, if only I'd looked.

'Oh, this amuses you does it?' he asks, his anger now at boiling point. 'Well, I have something even more amusing for you.'

Holding out a pair of scissors he begins to chop at my

hair. 'I told you, didn't I, that I prefer short hair on women! How many more times must you make me do this.'

Struggling against him, I wince as the scissors scrape across my forehead, causing a small shallow cut to open up. 'Get off me!' I scream, trying in vain to grab the scissors, ignoring the pain that shoots through my fingers as the blades slash at my skin, 'get the hell off me!'

'Not laughing now are you!'

Sobbing, I hang my head and look at the clumps of shorn hair that cover my lap. How could it have come to this again? How can one person destroy another in this way?

'Now tell me.' He whispers, kneeling before me, 'Tell me what you know about Amber.'

Shrugging, I pluck a long piece of hair from the floor, 'What does it matter now, she at least escaped you, you mad bastard!'

Standing, he slaps my face and drags me into the shower cubicle. I jump as cold water begins to rain down on me, washing away the blood from my face and the remnants of my beautiful hair.

'Tell me what you know or you stay in here until you do.'

Shivering now, I look up at him, this man that has destroyed every aspect of my life. 'Go to hell.'

'Jade? Are you in there?'

I must have fallen into unconsciousness because when I come to I hear banging on the front door and find Eric beside me with the scissors held to my throat.

Glancing into the bedroom I can see that I have been locked in here with Eric for nearly two hours. Jake must have been discharged and has now come to find me.

'Jade?' The letterbox rattles loudly through the oppressive silence of the house, 'Jade are you home?'

'One little peep and I'll make sure that these scissors cut you in places that even your nightmares couldn't imagine. Understand?'

Nodding, I pray for Jake to go away. I hope he thinks I've just left, that he doesn't continue knocking. God knows what Eric would do then.

'Looks like lover boy is looking for you. Planning your escape were you?'

Wrapping my arms around myself I find that I am unable to speak due to the chattering of my teeth. I don't know how long I've been under the cold water, but I am freezing through to my bones.

'Look I'm going to try the café again – Jade?'

Shivering, I ram my fist into my mouth so I don't scream out that I am here, I am home, yet another person that I

231

must save before myself.

'Cold?' Eric asks with a smirk, 'why don't I make you a deal. You tell me how you know about Amber, and I'll let you have a nice hot bath, oh, and I won't go downstairs and murder your little boyfriend. Deal?'

Nodding my head again, I watch as Eric begins to fill the bath, my body already reacting to the steam rising up from the taps. 'Thank you.' I murmur, between clenched teeth. Despite the abuse, despite the fear and hatred that I have for this man, I need his assistance right now, and as much as it pains me to be civil to him, I am just too cold to think straight.

'You see, Jade, it really isn't that difficult to be nice to me. Now, bubbles or no bubbles?'

'Bu...bub...bubbles please.'

'Wow, you really are cold. C'mon, let me help you in.'

Stripping off my sodden clothes I try not to recoil as Eric's gaze lingers on my bare breasts, 'You always did have an amazing body.' He grins as he helps me into the tub. 'perfection only ruined by that ugly scar on your leg. But we can get that fixed I'm sure.'

'I don't need fixing, it's proof that I survived.'

'Hmm, we'll see about that.'

Sinking beneath the bubbles and letting the hot water

soak into my frozen bones, I realise that the knocking has finally stopped.

'So, a deal is a deal, what do you know about Amber?'

He seems calm again as he washes my back, but it's all a disguise for the darkness that lurks so close to the surface, and I know how quickly that darkness takes over. If I tell him that Heidi told me, she will most certainly be on his hit list and I cannot do that to her.

'I read about her.' I lie, 'online.'

'Oh?'

'Yeah, the papers reported the incident, her picture was there, and yours.'

I know that I can't back any of this up, I know that if he decides to look himself he will see no such story, he will know that I am lying.

'And what did this newspaper say about the *incident.*

'Erm... just that you had had a disagreement, things got out of hand and you got into a fight.'

'Is that so?'

'Mmm.'

'And my parents? How do you know about them?'

'I, erm, found them, online.'

'Did you now?'

'Yep.'

'You see the thing is Jade, I believe you when you say that my parents have social media, everybody does, but what happened between Amber and I was never reported in any newspaper, I made sure of that. And she dropped any potential charges against me. So I ask again, how do you know about Amber?'

'I'd like to get out now.' I mumble, 'Could you help me please.'

'Of course.' He smiles, 'Once you keep to your end of the deal and tell me the truth.'

'I have.' I plead, 'I have told you the truth.'

'LIAR!'

Grabbing my shoulders he plunges me beneath the water, holding me there, and as I thrash about his grip only becomes tighter. I can't breathe and I'm not strong enough to push against him. This is how I'm going to die. It's not at all how I envisaged it.

Releasing his hold he lets me surface, and I grab as many lungfuls of air as I can manage, my eyes are burning from the soap and as I try to reach for a towel to wipe them he snatches it from me.

'Tell me how you know about Amber?'

'I've told you!' I scream, 'I'm not lying.'

Forcing me down once more I take a mouthful of air and

try to still my movements, I need to conserve energy, I need to be calm. I will not tell him that Heidi told me, I will not, I will take it to the grave with me, I will.

I can hear him speaking above me, it's garbled and incoherent, but it's no doubt the same words on repeat, *tell me what you know about Amber.*

Pulling me up, I once more gasp for breath, and am shocked to see him offer me a towel. I know that he is playing games with me, lulling me into a false sense of security, I've played this game many times and there is only ever one winner.

'Come on.' He beams, 'Let's get you tucked up in bed, nice and cosy.'

'But…'

'Don't worry.' He smiles, as I pull away from him, 'I know you'll tell me everything eventually.'

I don't want to go near any bed with him, but what choice do I have. Tucking me in, he declares that he is starving, that it has been one hell of a day, I hold back from retorting that he has no idea and instead suggest that I make him something to eat. If I can just get out of this bedroom I might stand half a chance of getting out of here alive, and Jake can't be too far away.

'Oh Jade, do you honestly think that I'm letting you

lose in the kitchen – you are a terrible cook.'

I was thinking more along the lines of the knives being in there and the front door not a million miles away, but I'm sure Eric is so secure in his belief that he has me running scared that he truly believes I will not try to escape.

I *am* petrified but I still have some fight left in me. I can't give up now.

'There's takeaway menus in the cupboard?' I suggest. Anything to get him out of this room.

'Yeah.' He laughs, 'That is definitely preferable. Now, you stay tucked up and I'll be right back.'

I don't immediately move when he leaves the room, unsure if it is one of his tests, but as I hear my early warning sign step give a little creak I fling myself from the bed and throw on dry jeans and a jumper. I don't have time to mess about with underwear or socks, so I just slip on my old battered trainers and make my way out onto the landing.

It's now or never. This may be the only chance that I get.

I can hear him moving about downstairs, opening cupboards, trying to find the menus, and cursing when he does not. I don't actually have any takeaway menus, so he might be looking for some time.

Moving slowly, I place my feet gently onto each step,

careful to avoid the one that creaks, careful not to make any sound at all. My heart feels as though it could beat right out of my chest, as blood pounds in my ears. I can see my suitcase by the door, but I know that attempting to leave with it would be a foolish move. I'll be quicker if it's just me.

I can see through to the kitchen now. Eric is scratching his head in confusion over where the blasted menus could be, and I know I don't have long until he admits defeat and heads back up the stairs to ask me.

Tiptoeing across to the front door I see that my keys are not in the lock. *Shit*! Did I lock it when I came in? No. I planned to just grab my suitcase and go, so it must still be open. Reaching out to try the door handle I hear a jangle behind me, and I close my eyes in defeat.

'Looking for these?' Turning I see Eric standing at the bottom of the stairs with my keys in his hands, a self-satisfied smirk on his face. 'I knew you'd try to leave, you are *so* predictable.'

'Just let me go, please.' I plead, 'We don't belong together, in your heart you know that.'

'You are mine, wife, you go where I tell you to go, and right now that would be back up those stairs.'

'I can't do that Eric. I can't be with you.'

'I don't recall you having a choice in the matter.'

Lunging for me he pins me against the front door, the handle digging painfully into my side, I can't be so close to escaping only to have it yanked away from me at the last hurdle.

'Get off me!' I yell, trying to push him away from me, 'I'm not staying here with you!'

Raising my knee I aim it straight for Eric's groin, and as he doubles over in pain I grab the keys and slide them into the lock. He's not down for long though and as he grabs the back of my jumper and pulls me down to the floor I am suddenly pinned. Sitting on my chest now, my breathing becomes laboured, my chest heaving as my body tries to drag in oxygen, he wraps his hands around my throat and begins to squeeze.

'It's such a cliché Jade.' He pants, 'But if I can't have you, then nobody can.'

I want to laugh then and if I weren't quite literally fighting for my life then I would. Could that one line be any more cheesy?

'Psycho!' I holler as I reach down and grab his balls through his jeans, twisting as hard as I can, 'get the fuck off me!'

Rolling away from him as he howls in pain, I reach for

the shelves by the door and grab the first thing to hand, a beautiful yet heavy vase that Dorothy bought for me as a welcome-to-Bardsey gift.

Smashing it over his head I sit back as he sways and then tries to reach for me once more. I have no choice but to hit him again. As blood appears on the side of his head and he falls against the wall, I leap to my feet, unlock the door and run out into the street. I should go back, and make sure he's really down this time, but I'm too afraid. I made that mistake once, and I won't be making it again.

Rushing past the village hall I try to cover my head and face as best as I can. I know what I must look like with my butchered hair and bloody face and hands, I just hope and pray that nobody sees me.

It isn't far to Jake's home, if I can just get there then I will be safe. We can grab his things and get going. I don't care that I have nothing but the clothes I'm standing in, I'm out of that house, I'm free once more and that is all that matters.

I dare not risk looking behind me. That is, in my opinion, always a great movie mistake. One that I used to scream at the TV about - just keep your eyes forward, don't trip, and don't stop. I would soon know about it if he were behind me, so why waste time looking.

Not that I have been a great advocate of what not to do in a movie. Grabbing that book was a huge error of judgment and one that I most certainly would have screamed at the TV about!

Rounding the corner now, I see Jake's lights are on, and as I pound on the door, trying to catch my breath, I swear I see a shadow moving towards me out of the corner of my eye.

Screaming now, I bang harder on the door.

'Jake! Let me in!'

The shadow is moving slowly, menacingly, is it him?

'Jake! Please, Jake!'

Glancing again at the shadow, I notice almost immediately that it is nothing but a silhouette of a big acorn tree blowing in the breeze. My nerves are frazzled, and as the door behind me is flung open I jump, letting out an involuntary screech.

'Jesus Christ Peyton, what the hell?' Wincing as Jake pulls me into his arms, I let myself, just for the briefest of moments, enjoy the warmth of him, 'I thought you'd gone, what the hell has happened to you? Where is he?' he growls.

Pulling out of his cosy embrace, I run shaking hands

through what is left of my hair, 'we need to go, now.'

'Tell me where he is.' Jake whispers, gently touching my cheek, 'I'll make him pay for this.'

'It doesn't matter, my hair will grow back.' I sob, 'My skin will heal, but please, can you just grab your stuff.'

'It's right here. But we need to call the police. If you won't let me find him, then we need to call them.'

'I will. I promise. Just as soon as we are aware from here. I need to go, Jake, are you coming with me, or not?'

Grabbing his bags from behind the door, he motions to my empty hands, 'Where are your things?'

'I had to leave them behind.' I say frantically, desperate to go now, 'I'll pick new stuff up later.'

'Well give me a second and I'll go over to your place and get them for you, it won't take me a minute.'

'NO! Jesus Jake, will you just listen to me, I need to go and I need to go now!'

I can't risk him walking into that house. I wouldn't be bothered if he discovered a dead body, I wouldn't even be bothered if he called the police and dobbed me in, but I would be bothered if there was no dead body and Eric was lying in wait for him. He's already made it perfectly clear what he thinks about my relationship with Jake, and I know exactly what he would do if he got his hands on him a second time.

'Please, I'm begging you. Can we just go?'

'Okay, okay.' He responds, frustrated, 'Let me just grab my car keys and we'll make a move. But really, you do need to tell me what is going on, how can I protect you if I don't know the full story.'

'Thank you.' I sigh, feeling all at once exhausted, 'and I will. I will tell you everything, just as soon as we are far away from here.'

I must have fallen asleep in the car because I am woken with a start by Jake tapping my shoulder.

'We're here sleepyhead.' He whispers, 'You want me to carry you in?'

'That's okay.' I yawn, rubbing sleep from my eyes, 'I can walk.'

The summer house is delightful. It's more of a cottage than the mac-mansion that I was expecting, but it looks to me as good as Buckingham Palace, it's perfect.

'We'll be safe here, nobody outside of my family knows about this place, so we won't be having any unexpected visitors.' Once inside he motions towards the bedroom, 'I think my mum might have a few bits of clothing in the wardrobe, jumpers, jeans that kind of thing. She's a tad larger than you, but if you can make do…'

Nodding wearily I smile my thanks, 'Would you mind at all if I just slept for a little while?' I yawn again, 'I'm sorry to bail on you, but I am just so bloody tired.'

'Not at all.' He nods, sympathetically. 'You catch some Z's and I'll see what I can rustle us up for tea.'

Reaching out for his hand, I give it a gentle squeeze. 'Thank you, Jake, for everything. I know that you must be confused, possibly even regretting getting involved with me at all, but I will explain everything to you. I will.'

'I know you will.' He beams at me, 'and just for the record, I don't regret a single thing. Now, sleep.'

Climbing beneath the thick duvet, I feel my eyes become heavier, the tension of the past few hours slipping away. How could this have happened again? Sure, I can understand that he found me, I always knew deep down that it was a possibility, but to watch me for so long and not act, for me to not have had even the tiniest of inklings that he was there fills me with a kind of fear that I cannot put into words.

I had thought that I was safe, I had believed that I had made a new life for myself, but he was there, he was always there, watching me, hating me, until he could watch no more.

Is he dead?

Am I a killer now?

My freedom may be short-lived. But I'll take it. If I have killed him, if I am now a murderer, then I will surely be punished. I will no doubt serve a hefty prison sentence for what I have done, despite what he has done to me over the years. I am sure that I will have my sympathisers, those that have also suffered at the hands of an abusive partner, but many, I am sure, will not understand. And why should they?

No matter the outcome, at least Eric Sawyer will never be able to harm anyone else ever again.

A week has somehow been and gone as Jake and I have settled into a relaxed and easy routine with one another. He has healed well after his attack and other than our popping out to the *Whiterose Shopping Centre* to pick up a few bits that I needed, we haven't ventured outside of the grounds at all.

The family summer house is located in East Keswick, another beautiful village, just as pretty as Bardsey, and is set in six acres of lush green gardens with breathtaking countryside views. We have spent many lazy hours wandering the grounds, picnicking, laughing, swapping tales of our childhoods and generally feeling free.

I explained to him why I needed to change my name and filled him in completely on the horrors that I have endured since meeting Eric, including his most recent attack on me and he was, naturally appalled and angry. I also told him how I left things the night that we left to come here. He agrees that if Eric is indeed dead, then it is something that we must inevitably face, together.

I hadn't expected him to want to stand by me, after all, who wants to be dragged into a potential murder investigation, but he said that he will stand by me every step of the way, and it's a feeling that I'm not at all used to.

We have decided, together, that we will head back to my house on Friday, two days from now, and confront whatever we may find lurking behind my front door. I'm petrified, but I can't avoid what I have done, any more than I can avoid the consequences of my actions.

I have two days of freedom left and I plan to make the most of them.

'Should we head back do you think?' Jake asks as he points to the clouds gathering overhead, 'looks like rain.'

We've had a lovely day, the weather has been

somewhat chilly, but wrapped up in our winter woollies we've not let it spoil the afternoon, instead, we have snuggled together on the picnic blanket under a big old tree and stuffed our faces with sandwiches, tea and cakes, it's been pure over-indulgent bliss.

'I think that's probably a good shout.' I smile, as I gather up the remnants of our cheap and cheerful al fresco dining. 'I'll get the hot chocolate on the go when we get back and you can pick a movie.'

'Deal. C'mon, let's get out of here before the heavens really open up.'

Gathering up the blanket and tucking it inside the picnic basket we make a run for it, just as the clouds decide to let loose their freezing cold globules and we are all at once drenched through.

'Aaargh!' I yell as icy cold droplets run down the back of my coat, 'it's freezing!'

'And you call yourself a Yorkshire lass.' Jake titters, as he yanks the blanket from the basket and drapes it over my head, 'Look, we're nearly there.'

Slipping and sliding on the sodden grass, we can't help but laugh hysterically as we try our hardest not to fall face-first into the mud beneath our feet.

Giggling, we tumble through the front door, out of breath,

rain dripping from our noses and eyelashes, 'That was a proper workout.' I gasp, 'I'm out of breath.'

Stripping out of our sopping clothes we both stand in our underwear shivering but still amused, and argue good-naturedly about who's hitting the shower first. Gentlemanly as always, Jake offers me first dibs, but as I sidle up close to him with a grin, I suggest that surely it's big enough for the both of us.

Taking my hand we sprint through the kitchen, pausing only to flick the heating on before we make a mad dash into the hallway.

Jake's hands are all over my body as I groan with undiluted pleasure and as he spins me around to face him, the passion that was only moments ago burning out of control is suddenly doused as I glance over his shoulder.

'What the...?' Totally unaware of my change in mood, Jake continues to seduce me, and as I feel his hand reach around to unclip my bra, I push him from me. 'Stop.' I whisper as I move away from him, 'There's something wrong.'

Confused, he looks to where I am pointing, not at all sure of what he is supposed to be looking at.

'What is it?'

'Oh god.' I gasp, 'Oh god.'

'Jade, you're scaring me. What's wrong?'

Stepping tentatively into the living room, my arms wrapped tightly around my shaking body, I point once more at the sofa, at the perfectly lined up cushions, all in a neat little row, all perfectly square.

'He's here.'

Pulling on jeans and my trusty battered trainers I rush past Jake and fling open the front door. It's still pouring down with rain, the sky dark and ominous, but I've had enough, if he's here then he might as well just get on with the job of finishing me off!

'What the hell are you doing Jade?' Jake shouts from behind me, 'It's chucking it down.'

Ignoring him I run out into the garden, 'Eric! I know you're here! Why don't just come out you coward, stop hiding! ERIC!'

'Jade, for crying out loud, get back inside, it's freezing.'

'Eric!' I yell again as I frantically poke around in the bushes, 'Get out here now! You can't keep doing this to me. I do not love you, can you get that through your thick skull. I hate you!'

'I'm calling the police.' Jake mutters behind me, 'This is madness.'

'Don't you dare.' I bark, pointing my finger at him, 'This is between me and my psycho soon-to-be *very* ex-husband!'

'This is crazy, you are acting crazy, there is nobody here.'

'I am not crazy!'

'Jade, right now you are!'

'Don't you get it?' I shout, 'This is what he does, this he how he torments me. He's here. Trust me.'

'I think we should call the police. If he is here then they can handle it.'

Ignoring him, I scream as loud as I can, 'You want me dead Eric? Then get out here and do it, you coward!'

A shadow moves to the left of me, and despite being afraid, I stand my ground.

'I don't want you dead, *wife*.' Eric snarls as he moves slowly towards me, 'I want you back where you belong.'

'As your prisoner?'

'You know Jade.' He smirks, 'It's interesting that you despise me and yet you fall for a man just like me.'

'Jake is nothing like you!' I spit. '*Nothing*.'

'Are you sure about that? You see, I broke into *his* house, found the address for this place easily enough, and do you know what else I found, wife?'

'Oh, do enlighten me.'

'He's neat, Jade. Everything is just so tidy. Quite the opposite of you, wouldn't you say.'

'Is that the best you've got? Jake is tidy? That hardly makes him like you now does it!'

'I wonder though, why you haven't been permitted to see inside his extremely organised home?'

'What?'

'Not even when you ran to him, Jade. Bleeding, upset, scared. He still left you standing on the doorstep. Don't you find that just a little odd?'

'I find *you* odd, Eric. Look at you, big man, trying to undermine my relationship with someone decent, caring, and kind. It won't work. I'm not going anywhere with you, you'll have to kill me first!'

'I wasn't intending for things to end this way.' He frowns, 'but if they must…'

'Jade, get back inside, now!' Jake hollers from somewhere behind me. 'I'll handle this.'

As Jake and Eric race towards each other, I am flung sideways. Losing my balance I fall to the ground, my knee connecting painfully with the tarmac drive. Howling in pain, I watch in horror as Eric's first punch connects viciously with Jake's forehead.

Jake however is undeterred as he rugby tackles Eric to the

ground, raining punches down on his face. The fight is savage and I know if Eric gains ground on Jake then he will surely kill him.

'You can't have her!' Jake roars, 'She's mine!'

Dragging myself across the tarmac, away from the violence, my leg throbbing and weak, I freeze at Jake's words. *She's mine.* Staring at the battle before me I know that surely his words must have been said in the heat of the moment. I belong to nobody. He knows that. And yet... he still said them.

Reaching for one of many decorative stones that line the driveway I scramble across to where Eric has thrown Jake from his chest and is now towering above him. Lifting the stone high I bring it crashing down onto Eric's head. He wails in pain as I try to bring the rock back up again, but the rain has made it too slippery to hold, and as it slips from my fingers I feel the full force of Eric's fist hit my cheek.

Screaming, I try to pull myself away from him, but I'm dizzy, the rain has made my clothes heavy and I know that I am losing strength. As Eric raises his hand once more, I brace myself for the impact that will undoubtedly render me unconscious, but the hit does not come.

Blinking rain out of my eyes I see Jake hovering above

Eric, the bloodied rock in his hand, and Eric lying motionless beneath him.

'Is he…?'

Jake lifts the rock again and pummels Eric's face, the sound making me gag, 'Yeah, he is.' Jake whispers, 'For good this time.'

As darkness descends, my panic rises.

'What are we going to do with the body?' I ask Jake, as we dry ourselves off, 'We can't leave him out there. Should we call the police now?'

'No, not yet, I need to think.'

'But..'

'Can you just let me think, please! Jesus Jade!'

Jake has covered Eric's body with some old tarpaulin that he found in the garage, and the rain has done a good enough job of washing away the blood that was oozing from his face and head during the attack. But we both know that he can't stay out there forever.

'I've had an idea.' Jake says calmly, which unnerves me slightly, he has after all just killed a man, and yet, you would think we were discussing how to get rid of an old washing machine. 'There's an old well not far from here, that hasn't been used in years, we could…'

'Oh god.' I groan, 'Put him in there? Just dump him?'

'You got any better ideas?'

'Well, no, I...'

'Right then, the well it is.'

'But how will we get him there? Where is it exactly?'

I'm a nervous wreck. Men like Eric don't just vanish – questions will be asked. The police will track his car, his mobile phone, and his bank cards. It's hopeless.

'There's a sledge in the garage, we can use that to transport the body and then it's just a matter of leverage.'

'Leverage?' I squeak.

'Look you're injured.' He smiles sadly at my leg, 'I can take care of this on my own if you don't feel up to it. You just have yourself a hot bath, relax and let me deal with this.'

'I can't leave you to *deal with this*, Jake. You're only in this crazy situation because of me. Just tell me what I need to do.'

The sledge is cumbersome as we struggle to pull it across the muddy fields to the rear of the summer house, and my leg throbs with the pain of an old injury reignited.

'How far is it?' I yell over the howling wind that seems to

253

have picked up immensely since we were last outside.

'Not far now. It's just beyond those trees over there.'

He points ahead, but all I can see are trees, trees and more bloody trees, so I'm not exactly sure which ones he is referring to.

'Look, you go back if you're not up to it.'

'I'm fine thank you.' I snap, fed up now with this sledge and the mud and the never-ending trees. 'Let's just get it done.'

Slipping in the mud, I find myself suddenly falling, unable to get any grip on the ground at all, and as I land face down on Eric's stiff body I let out a cry of horror.

'Jesus, Jade.' Jake bawls at me, 'Could you make any more noise!'

'Do you maybe want to help me?' I shout back, 'Or do you want to drag us both to the bloody well!'

'I knew I should have done this by myself.' He mutters as he hauls me back up onto my feet, 'You're slowing us down.'

'Oh really, have somewhere else you need to be do you?'

'Look, it's just over there, do you think you can manage to stay upright until then?'

I know it's just the situation that we are in that is making both of us irate, but I really do hate being snapped at, so ignoring his raised eyebrow I begin to pull the sledge once more, this time with even more determination.

This whole situation is just insane. Who in their right mind drags a dead body through the mud and rain and darkness to dump them into a disused well for crying out loud. This is the sort of thing they make documentaries about. The sort of creepy fascination that people like me binge-watch on *Netflix*! It is not what normal people do.

Normal people call the police.

Normal people face facts and fess up.

They do not bludgeon someone to death and hide the body in the middle of the bloody night!

Blinded by the rain I do not see the well despite being almost upon it, 'we're here.' Jake murmurs, 'This is it.'

'Oh.' I whisper, suddenly unsure of what happens next, 'Right. Okay.'

The well is deep from what I can make out in the darkness, and just as Jake described it doesn't look like it has been used for a very long time.

'This well isn't on any of the ordinance maps, so nobody knows it even exists outside of my family. I think the previous owners must have built it themselves.'

'So, your family *and* the previous owners know about it then.'

'They would if they were still alive.'

'Oh.'

'I'll get the head end, that's always the heaviest, are you alright grabbing his legs?'

I don't want to. I don't ever want to touch Eric Sawyer again, but I can see that I have little choice in the matter.

'Do you erm... you know... want to say a few words.' Jake asks, nervously.

'Absolutely not!' I fume, 'What could I possibly say?! Sorry, you were such a bastard and we had to kill you?'

'Okay, no need for sarcasm.'

'There's every need, Jake. Look at what we're doing! Can we just get him in?'

With a lot of muscle power and sweat, we manage to get Eric's body halfway over the lip of the well, and with one final push, he drops into the seemingly never-ending darkness below.

I don't know what I expected to feel.

Guilt maybe?

Sadness?

But I feel none of those things, and as I peer into the gloom below me, I am overcome suddenly by euphoria.

It's over. He's gone.

Even Eric Sawyer could not come back from this.

'**W**hat will I say.' I begin, wringing my hands, 'If the police ask me? What will I say?'

We've been back an hour or so now and the implications of what we have just done are finally starting to sink in.

'You say nothing. You have no link to this place, nobody knows about our relationship outside of the village and they all think we broke up after the fete anyway. Trust me, they will never find the body and they will never suspect *you*.'

Why wouldn't they suspect me? I think to myself. I'm the battered wife, I'm the one with the motive. I will absolutely be the first person that they suspect. But, why would it just be *me* that they were suspicious of?

Should he not have said they won't suspect *us*?

Surely the police would never believe that I was capable of dragging a man, a 6ft 3 man at that, through the mud and rain only to then dump him into a well all by myself!

Would Jake pin it all on me if push came to shove?

I can't help but think back, uncharitably, to Eric's words, *'Not even when you ran to him, Jade. Bleeding, upset, scared. He still left you standing on the doorstep. Don't you find that just a little odd?'* I know that Eric was just trying to hurt me, and cast doubt on my relationship with Jake, but why didn't he let me in?

257

Is he hiding something from me?

Eric was right though, I have never seen the inside of Jake's house, he never asked me back there, he never suggested we meet there, he didn't invite me in when I was bleeding and hurt.

Could it be possible that he has something, some side of him that he does not want me to see?

He was a little peculiar when he said that just leaving the hospital wasn't orderly, and he did initially find Eric's OCD amusing when I told him about it. But does that make him the same as Eric?

I'm reluctant to tar him with the same brush, but what if Eric recognised himself in Jake. What if Eric knew because it takes one to know one?

Glancing at myself in the hallway mirror I don't recognise the woman that stares back at me. The woman that made a plan, that ran through Whitby, jumped onto an opening swing bridge and begged her way onto a bus.

The woman that did all of those things is not the one looking back at me with haunted eyes and patchy hair. She is long gone, and I fear that the Jade of old is slipping even further away from me.

I know that I am free now.

I know that I can finally return to Whitby. I can pick my life back up, I can clear my house of everything Eric and start afresh.

I cannot wait to hug my parents, drink and dance until I drop at *The Dirty Rabbit*, re-grow my hair, wear red lipstick, have a social media account, take stupid selfies and count my likes. I cannot wait to go home!

But never will I forget what I have done tonight.

Never will I forget Eric's glassy eyes staring out at me from the tarpaulin, and never will I forget how it felt to see him fall to the bottom of that well.

It felt good and I don't know if that makes me a terrible person, I don't know if I'm allowed to feel elated, to feel happiness that he is gone. But I do.

I don't know how Jake will react when I tell him that I am going home. I hope that he will be supportive. I hope that he will understand why I must. I hope tonight's events do not plague him to such a degree that he is unable to live with the guilt. I cannot let him confess, I will not let him ruin the only chance of happiness that I have left.

'Do you want a cup of tea?' I call out to Jake, as I make my way up the stairs to the bedroom, 'I'm going to have another one.' He does not respond, and as I push open the door to the bedroom he is still oblivious to my presence.

What is he doing?

Leaning in I watch in horror as Jake lines up the ties in his wardrobe in perfect alignment with his shirts.

Turning quietly I back out of the bedroom, only to find the one floorboard that creaks. His head whips around then and he sees me. 'Oh, there you are. I was wondering what was taking so long. Did you do this with my ties?'

'No.' I whisper, 'You did, I just saw you.'

'I didn't. I just came up here and found them like this. I thought maybe you were playing a prank on me.'

'And why would I do that? Why would I do one of the many things that have haunted my life for years, as a prank?'

'Maybe you didn't know you were doing it?' he suggests, a strange smile playing on his lips.

'What's going on Jake.' I ask, confused. 'why have you done this?'

'I haven't done anything.' He argues, 'If it wasn't you then it must have been Eric.'

I can't explain at all why I don't believe him. Why I am certain that he is lying. It is totally conceivable that Eric could have done this, he did after all rearrange the cushions on the sofa, but, if it was Eric, then why didn't

Jake alert me immediately to his discovery, why was he just standing there, looking at the ties and the shirts, looking smug, looking pleased with himself?

'Why didn't you let me into your house, Jake?' I question, desperate for any answer that will dispute Eric's accusations, '*Are* you hiding something from me?'

'You're acting crazy Jade! There is no mystery. We always just met at your place or the pub – you never once expressed an interest in seeing inside my home. Look...' He smiles, taking my hands in his, '...he's just making you paranoid, can't you see that?'

'But what about that last night? The night I escaped? I was hurt and bleeding and you just left me standing on the doorstep.'

'You were the one that wanted to leave Jade! You wouldn't even let me go back to your house and get your things. He's inside your head, nothing is going on here, I swear! Can you not trust me, even now? I killed a man for you tonight and still you question me?'

'For *me*?' I fume, yanking my hands out of his, 'You killed him for *you* because it was either you or him. Don't you dare say you killed him for me! He was practically unconscious Jake, we could have restrained him and called the police, but no, you bashed his head in!'

'For you!' he roars, pacing the floor, 'if he'd killed me, then what? Do you think he would have dusted himself off, had a nice cup of tea and then driven you back to Whitby? No! He'd have killed you too Jade. So yeah, I did it for you!'

'Well, I never asked you to.'

'You wish I'd restrained him? So you could have him arrested, and take him to court? We both know that you never would have done that, you would never have been brave enough to see that through.'

'You have no idea how brave I am. I've survived this long, without your help! You know nothing about me.'

'Maybe you're right.' He shrugs as he sits down on the bed, 'but what in all honesty do you know about me? We need to trust one another, now more than ever, because if either one of us cracks then we automatically take the other one down with us, is that what you want?'

'I won't crack.' I snap back at him, 'But how do I know you won't let the side down?'

'You don't. That's generally how trust works.'

How can I trust that six months down the line Jake won't be riddled with guilt at his part in the murder and disposal of my husband?

How can I leave him with the power to destroy me?

262

'I'm going to be heading back to Whitby tomorrow, try and pick up the remnants of my life there. I think it's best if I go alone.'

'Oh.' He frowns, 'And when did you decide this?'

'Does it matter?'

'Yeah, I think it does matter, actually. Don't you think it's going to look a bit strange that you return just as your husband vanishes?'

'I'll just have to deal with any questions as and when they arise. I can't keep running forever.'

'And what about us? How will we survive the distance?'

'It isn't far from here to Whitby.' I laugh.

'I meant the emotional distance as you very well know. You settle back into your old life and I just what? Hang around waiting for you to remember that I exist?'

'I have to go home Jake, that's the only thing that has kept me going all these years, knowing that one day I would go home. You're being a little selfish and needy right now.'

'Selfish?' he scoffs, 'selfish? When I have ever not put you first?'

'It isn't a case of putting me first! I need to go home!'

'Then go.' He sulks. 'just go, leave me.'

I know then that Jake will most certainly crumble. That the knowledge of what we have done here tonight will eat away at him until he cannot handle the pressure any longer. At that moment, all of the fighting that I have done to be free will have been for nothing.

I should have known that Jake's abandonment issues would be a problem, I only need to think back to the weeks before the fete when he bombarded me with calls and texts. How angry he was that I had not responded to him. Him screaming that I belong to him. Can I really trust that our being apart now, after all of that we have done, will be any easier for him?

He will panic, he will worry that I have forgotten about him, and he will be so consumed with paranoia that he will crack and confess to everything.

Jake is the weak link.

'We don't have to let this ruin our last night together.' I smile seductively, 'and we won't be apart for long, I promise.' Taking a deep breath I casually walk into the ensuite bathroom, undressing as I go and look over my shoulder at him, 'Are you coming?' I smile, as I reach out and turn on the shower, slyly swiping a pair of scissors from the side of the sink.

'I would have thought you'd be too tired.' He grins as he hurriedly pulls his clothes off, his sulking from only moments ago all but forgotten.

'I'm never too tired for that.' I purr, as I wrap my arms around him and pull him into the shower with me.

As Jake begins to lather my body with soap, I take the scissors and plunge them deep into the side of his neck, watching with fascination as his face first registers the assault and his body then reacts to it.

'Jade?' he gurgles, as blood fills his mouth, 'What have you done?'

Smiling sadly, I look at him, this man that I thought would be different, this man that I thought I could have some kind of future with and I shake my head, 'I stopped you from hurting me.' I shrug, as he crumples to the floor of the shower, 'I just can't go through this again, I hope you can understand that.'

His death doesn't take long at all, and maybe I am wrong about him, maybe I have made yet another mistake, but, as I watch his blood flow down the plughole I know that I have done the right thing. Why take the risk? Haven't I done that too many times already?

Haven't I lived on somebody else's terms for too long?

And my therapist did say that *my* life should be on *my* terms, though I think maybe I'll leave this little incident out of our next session.

It's poetic, the way that this has ended. Here in this

shower cubicle, the blood, the scissors, the violence – all of the things that I have suffered many times over in this very situation – it was inevitable really.

I wanted to kill Damon, but I didn't.

I wanted to kill Eric, but I didn't.

I never wanted to hurt Jake and yet I have.

They all hurt me in one way or another and there is only so much one person can take.

The blood, the scissors, the violence.

Sliding down the glass of the shower cubicle, I cradle Jake's head in my arms, 'I'm sorry.' I sob as I touch his face with shaking hands, 'I just want to go home. It's all I've ever wanted.'

I don't know how long has passed, sitting here, apologising to Jake, crying with both sadness and relief, struggling to comprehend all that has happened since meeting Eric, the way that he has utterly devastated my life, but as I kiss Jake's forehead one last time and scramble ungracefully from beneath him, I know that I need to make a plan.

I need to call the police. Tell them that Eric attacked us, that Jake killed him to protect me. But, how do I then explain Jake's death? It would seem unlikely that he killed a man to save me, only to turn on me himself.

No.

I need to hide Jake's body. He's smaller than Eric, so I should be able to take him to the well myself.

I never wanted it to end this way, two men dead, killed because of me and I don't know how this will affect me in the long run, but I do know one thing with absolute certainty - I'm going home.

Acknowledgements

I would like to first thank my husband, Paul, for the many many hours that he has listened to me talking crazy, plotting and scheming and possibly driving him mad.

(is that even possible!)

Also and more importantly for driving me to Whitby so that we could plan and walk Jade's escape route – those 199 steps were a killer! But, the fish and chips at the end were totally worth it.

Also *(yes, yes I know he's a long-suffering husband)*, for calling me mid-write to tell me he'd found the perfect location for Jade's new life, Bardsey, and for taking me there so that we could walk around and map out the next stages of the story.

Thank you to the owners of Castlegate Cottage, who may or may never know that their beautiful home is the setting of Jade's cottage in Bardsey.

I would like to thank my mum, Anne, for her endless support and for always believing in me.

Thank you also to my wonderful readers, you are the absolute best for taking time out to read my ramblings, I hope that you enjoyed them.

Dear Reader

Thank you for purchasing NOW YOU SEE ME…

I know that there are many other books that you could have picked to read and I am extremely grateful that you selected mine.

I hope that you enjoyed sharing Jade's journey with me, and like me, you laughed, cried and screamed at the pages, praying for her to finally make it home.

I would love to hear from you, and if you would be kind enough to leave me a review on Amazon or Goodreads then it would really make my day.

All feedback is greatly appreciated.

Thank you again for taking the time to read my book.

www.emmalbealauthor.com

Facebook: Emma L Beal – Author

Goodreads: Emma L. Beal

Instagram: @emmalbeal

BOOK CLUB QUESTIONS

Which scene stuck with you the most?

If you could ask the author anything, what would it be?

How did this book impact you?

What most surprised you about this book?

Did the book feel real to you?

If you were the neighbours, what would you have done?

Did you race to the end, eager to know if Jade eventually made it home?

Did you agree with Jade's decisions?

What is the most important point the author makes in this book?

Would you read another book by this author?

COMING SOON

PART 2

NOW YOU DON'T

Whitby, North Yorkshire – idyllic, peaceful, picturesque, the perfect place to hide a secret?

An escape that ended in two men dead.
A woman hiding the deadliest of secrets.

When Jade Locke finally escaped the clutches of her abusive husband Eric, she never expected that one day she would be hiding his body, along with that of her lover, Jake, in a disused well.
But freedom was all that mattered to Jade. All she ever wanted was to go home.
She would not allow anyone to take that from her, no matter the cost.
So, when the first of many letters arrive from a stranger, professing to know exactly what she did in East Keswick, Jade has to wonder, just who has been watching her, and who can she really trust?

Can Jade's secret truly stay hidden forever?

Sneak Preview

NOW YOU DON'T

My home.

My sanctuary.

Everything in here is tainted.

How could I now be free, only to feel trapped once more by such a sense of desolation?

Eric isn't here, and yet, I feel him all around me.

I met Eric Sawyer in the May of 2019 – a chance meeting really as I hadn't intended to go out that evening. I had sworn off men forever, but, Heidi, my best friend persuaded me to slip on my best *catch-a-fella* outfit and head to *The Dirty Rabbit* for a few cheeky drinks, and meet him I did. Do I have wonderful memories of that first encounter?

No.

I don't have any wonderful memories of the man that would quickly become my husband, because he's tainted them all with his violence and his hatred. Anything sweet at the start of our relationship quickly spoiled. Everything that I stupidly perceived to be happiness suddenly turned sour and went bad.

Eric was bad.

My friends warned me about him, begged me to leave, they tried to save me, they really did. But I was stupid, I believed he loved me. I was wrong and they, unfortunately, were right.

Eric's violence in our marriage escalated to such extreme levels that I knew one day he would kill me. Everything that I did was wrong. The way I dressed, the way I behaved, the way I prepared his coffee or shut the blinds, absolutely every little thing, no matter how small, how insignificant, was wrong. And for those errors, I was punished.

Would our marriage have survived, and been somewhat normal if I'd watched my tone of voice? Agreed with everything he said and did? If I'd initiated sex more, despite my revulsion to have his hands anywhere near me? Would it have been better if I had been the *perfect* wife? Would it? No! I could have been the epitome of perfection and it still wouldn't have been enough.

Looking back over the years that have passed with my rose-tinted glasses long removed, I can see now what my friends saw. I can admit that the way he treated me was wrong. But back then I would not have heard a bad word said about him. How stupid I was. How wrapped up in the fantasy that I wanted so desperately.

I do see it now.

I knew after the car accident that left me wheelchair-bound that I needed to escape, so I plotted in secret. I had learnt to walk again. I had such an overwhelming desire to live that even the thought of being caught fleeing would not deter me from trying. And I *had* beaten him. Despite him telling me over and over that I belonged to him, that I could never leave. I had. I had dragged my broken body through Whitby and I had escaped.

Of course, my futile attempts at a new life in Bardsey, with a shiny new name were to be short-lived. I knew he wouldn't let me be. I knew that he would use all of his resources to find me. And that's exactly what he did.

After only three (of the best) years, he tracked me down, and the freedom that I so desperately cherished was once again snatched from me in the cruellest of ways.

There was a new man in my life by that point. A man that I had ever so slightly fallen for. Jake was the polar opposite of Eric (or so I had believed), and Eric in a jealous rage had beaten him almost to a pulp. He told me that I was never to see him again.

Of course, in the way that things always go with Eric, the situation escalated quickly. Despite once again being held captive in my own home, despite being broken and humiliated, I had beaten him at his own game once more and fled into the night with a rather confused and angry Jake. Our bliss however was once again shattered by Eric's arrival at Jake's parent's summer house. Eric would just not let me be free. He didn't know how to let go of his 'possession'.

That night ended badly.

Eric was dead. Murdered by Jake.

Jake was dead. Murdered by me.

Less than one week ago Jake beat my husband to death and between us, we dropped his dead body into a disused well.

That same night I killed Jake. It wasn't an accident; it was very much intentional. I needed to be free, I wanted to go home and he was hindering my new life. I truly had no choice.

If you could only comprehend what I have suffered, if you could only feel for one brief moment a third of what I have endured, you would have done the same.

Wouldn't you?

Eric and I never had the perfect marriage, it wasn't ever the fairy tale that I had hoped for, but for two men to now be dead because of me is something that I need to learn to live with. It's something that I need to accept. Eric was evil and he didn't deserve to live. But Jake?

Poor Jake was just weak. If I could have trusted him, if I could have had faith, just a tiny amount of faith, that he wouldn't jeopardise my freedom, then he would still be alive today. But I had no faith and I could not risk him confessing to what we had done.

I just wanted to go home.

My husband was evil and now he's dead. I may not have delivered that fatal last blow, but I wish I had.

Three days have passed since I left Bardsey.

Three days since I dragged Jake's lifeless body through the mud and the rain and dumped his corpse into the disused well at his family's summer house, alongside my abusive husband Eric.

Three days since I scrubbed that house of all trace of me. I cleaned away the broken vase that I beat Eric with, scooped up what remained of my beautiful hair, tidied the bedroom and washed the sheets, I scrubbed until blisters formed on my hands and then and only then did I allow myself a moment to just sit in silence, to just breathe.

Three days of wondering if I was doing the right thing. Should I confess, hand myself into the police and own up to my part in the death of these men?

Three days of convincing myself that I did the right thing. The only thing that I could do.

Three days since I packed what few belongings I had and made my way back home, back to Whitby.

And now, here I am, surrounded by the walls that were my sanctuary for the longest time, a sanctuary that quickly became a prison. A prison that I had to fight to break free from.

I met Eric in the May of 2019 and finally escaped his evil clutches in the October of 2022 – now, December 2025, I cannot at all comprehend how I have survived the past six years. How I can be back here where it all started. Changed and yet still somehow standing.

I had been scared and nervous as I approached the door that I fled from. Not because I feared a surprise, I of all people knew that Eric was absolutely not waiting to ambush me. But, because of all the memories that would come flooding back in an overwhelming avalanche of distress the moment I saw inside again. I was not wrong.

Everything is just how I left it.

The plant pot by the front door where I would hide the books that Eric forbade me to read. The Tampax box in the bathroom where I hid the pill from Eric is still undiscovered. The cans in the cupboard are still lined up, the clothes in the wardrobe are still ordered by colour and the place is immaculate. As I knew it would be.

Eric would never have it any other way.

The rooms, however, no matter how tidy, and how organised, still for me, harbour the darkest of memories.

The kitchen where he first raised his fist to me because I dared to mock his OCD, it had been a joke and yet that moment had set so many other things in motion.

The table where he threw coffee in my face, the floor where he beat me as though I were nothing. The bedroom, oh god, the bedroom. His abuse, his relentless sexual assaults, the way he threatened to kick the bathroom door down as I hid, terrified and alone. The horrors that these walls have seen and heard cannot accurately be put into words.

How can I bear to be back here?

How I can step through the front door and hope to try and live here again?

Because I have nothing else. That's how.

Pushing open the door to the spare bedroom, I gasp as I see the wheelchair that I had needed during my convalescence, sitting proudly in the centre of the room. It now has ankle and wrist restraints, proving in the simplest of visual ways that Eric evidently had plans for my return, and they most certainly included blocking any future escape attempts.

If I weren't already convinced that his death was the best outcome for that madman, then I sure do now. Can you just imagine what my life would have been like had I returned with him?

The past would seem like a walk in the park.

Nobody knows that I am back. My best friend Heidi should have been the first person that I told, she has, after all, been there for me every step of the way. But to tell her that I am home would warrant an explanation of how that is even possible. She would ask about Eric, and even though I know that she would understand eventually, I just do not have it in me at this time to tell her what happened three nights ago. I can scarcely believe it myself.

I also know that I need to see my parents, who again, will ask after Eric.

So many questions and so few answers.

I just need time. I just need to be alone for a little while.

To comprehend all that has happened. To get my story straight. Because even if I do tell my friends and my parents, I can never ever tell anyone else.

All they will see is a murderer.

They will not see a survivor.

I'll be dragged through the courts; the newspapers will have a field day and some lucky reporter will finally get his or her 'big break'.

My family and friends will be hounded, and every post I've ever made, shared, or liked on social media will be scrutinised!

Did anyone see this coming?

What's the real truth of Jade Locke – was she the victim or the instigator?

Is there any actual evidence that I was a beaten wife? Other than the testimonies of my friends, Heidi especially, there will be nothing. Not one tangible scrap of proof that I was indeed the victim.

And then will come the ultimate finale, after being grilled for hours in the police station in a t.v-esque good cop, bad cop routine, I will finally cave and admit to everything, and that is when they will find the bodies!

Eric's head smashed in, Jake's throat slashed open, a post-mortem will reveal it all, and I will be branded a ruthless killer. A maniac on a killing spree. A man-hater.

So, no one can ever know outside of those that I truly trust. This secret must remain watertight.

But, can secrets like this really stay secrets forever?

NOW YOU DON'T
COMING SOON

FOLLOW ME ON FACEBOOK

'Emma Beal – Author'

FOR MORE BOOK UPDATES

Printed in Great Britain
by Amazon